...ART

and the Zintrepids

Book 1

The Zintrepids

Alain M. Bergeron
Illustrated by Sampar

Translated by Sophie B. Watson

ORCA BOOK PUBLISHERS

Cataloguing in Publication information available from Library and Archives Canada

Issued in print and electronic formats.
ISBN 978-1-4598-1837-8 (softcover).—ISBN 978-1-4598-1838-5 (pdf).—
ISBN 978-1-4598-1839-2 (epub)

First published in the United States, 2018
Library of Congress Control Number: 2018933707

Summary: In this illustrated novel for middle-grade readers, Billy Stuart and his loyal Scout group get lost on a hike and inadvertently travel through time.

Orca Book Publishers gratefully acknowledges the support for its publishing programs provided by the following agencies: the Government of Canada through the Canada Book Fund and the Canada Council for the Arts, and the Province of British Columbia through the BC Arts Council and the Book Publishing Tax Credit.

We acknowledge the financial support of the Government of Canada through the National Translation Program for Book Publishing, an initiative of the *Roadmap for Canada's Official Languages 2013-2018: Education, Immigration, Communities*, for our translation activities.

Cover and interior illustrations by Sampar
Translated by Sophie B. Watson

ORCA BOOK PUBLISHERS
orcabook.com

Printed and bound in China.

21 20 19 18 • 4 3 2 1

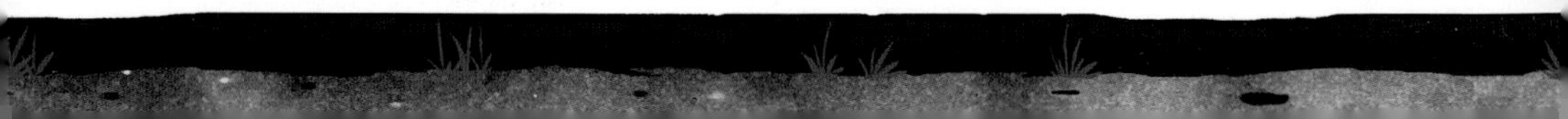

Table of Contents

Characters 6

Dear Reader 7

Chapter 1: Our Darling FrouFrou 9

Get Lost! 18

Chapter 2: Enough Is Enough! 21

Chapter 3: A Letter from My Grandfather 31

Chapter 4: When Tomorrow Is Today 41

Do You Know Your Colors? 48

Chapter 5: The Zintrepids' Anthem 53

Chapter 6: Beware the Grouchy Bear 63

Topsy-Turvy 74

Chapter 7: In Belcher's Cavern 75

Chapter 8: Operation Get Us Out of Here! 85

Who Am I? 94

Chapter 9: On the Right Track? 95

Chapter 10: On the Other Side of the Wall 103

Chapter 11: Unexpected Reunions 113

Chapter 12: "Scriiiii!" 117

Chapter 13: Batman 123

Tongue Twisters 128

Chapter 14: Daemon-Bat! 129

Chapter 15: A Bridge-Quake 135

A Puzzle 150

Chapter 16: Back in the Open Air 151

Search and Find 156

Solutions 158

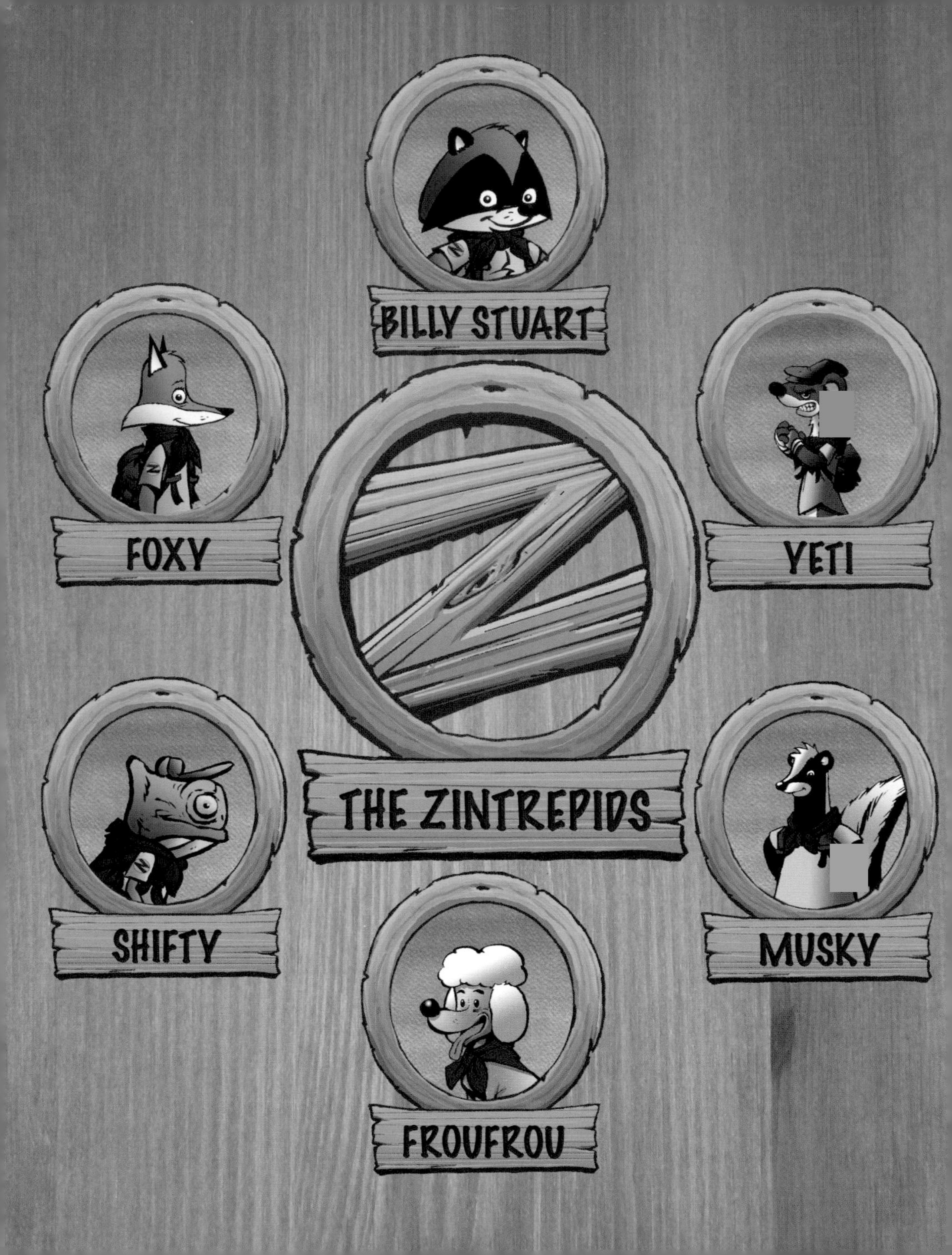
BILLY STUART
FOXY
YETI
THE ZINTREPIDS
SHIFTY
MUSKY
FROUFROU

DEAR READER,

Billy Stuart wasn't exactly elected to this particular position. He doesn't wear a magical ring on his finger like Frodo. He doesn't have a secret collection of masks or stones hidden in his drawers like Zelda. He hasn't walked through life accompanied by a daemon like Lyra. Nor does he have a distinctive lightning-shaped scar on his forehead like Harry. Basically, the future of the world does not rest on his thin and bony shoulders.

Billy Stuart is just a young, ordinary raccoon who has experienced some extraordinary adventures.

Here is the first adventure he told me about.

Alain M. Bergeron

One twelfth of January, in the town of Cavendish.

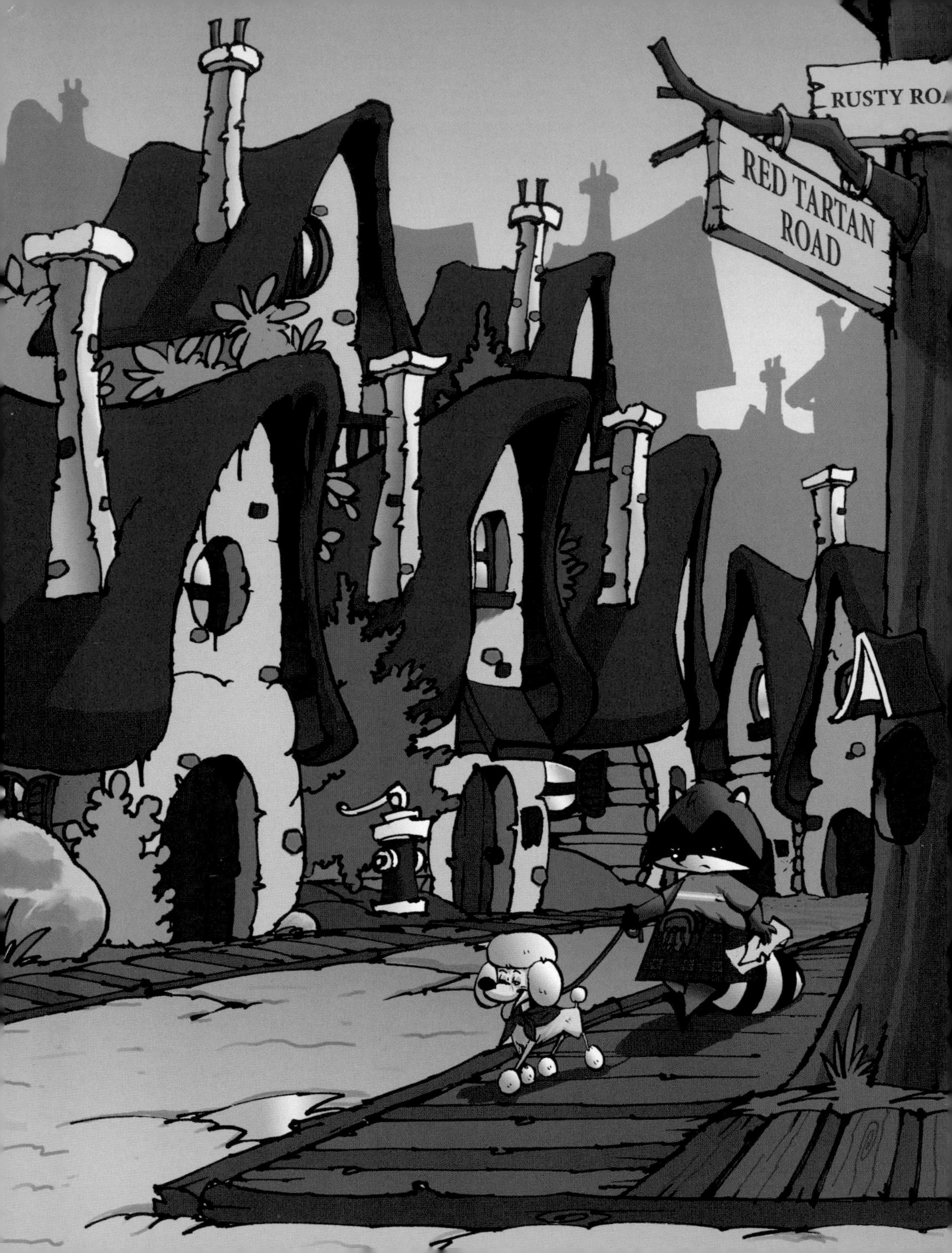
RUSTY ROA
RED TARTAN ROAD

Chapter 1

Our Darling FrouFrou

In the pretty town of Cavendish where I live—me, Billy Stuart—the sidewalks are made out of **WOOD** and the roads are made of **dirt**. Around here, all the houses on each road are the same color. I live on Red Tartan Road. The red tartan represents the Stuart family. I have lots of friends who also live in the neighborhood:

- **Foxy,** the fox, on the Rusty Road;
- **Musky,** the skunk, on the Black and White Road;
- **Yeti,** the weasel, on the White Road in the winter and the Brown Road in the summer;
- **Shifty,** the chameleon, on the MULTICOLORED Road, depending on the tint of the sky. Today his house is azure blue, because it's a beautiful day out there.

Unfortunately for me, there's no storm in the forecast. I'm supposed to go walk the dog, FrouFrou. I can only take him out on sunny days. Otherwise he would smell like wet dog, and it would ruin his beautiful fur coat. Where is the rain when I need it?

FrouFrou is a white poodle whom I detest. He belongs to the MacTerrings, our neighbors. At the beginning of the summer I had the brilliant idea to offer them my dog-walking services in exchange for a few bucks. They eagerly accepted. This provides me with a bit of pocket money to go to the shop on Candy Road to get my favorite treat— chocolate-covered crawfish!!!

Yummy, yummy, yummy! So delicious!!

And now it's been weeks that I've been walking ol' FrouFrou. No crawfish, not even chocolate-dipped ones, are worth this effort!

First of all, what he looks like. FrouFrou is a classic poodle—his **body** is all shaved, except for his **paws**, his **neck**, his **head** and his **tail**.

It's totally ridiculous.

If only that was all. But his attitude, his high-and-mighty attitude! His kennel is almost as **BIG** as our house! As soon as he puts one paw outside, this high-class dog transforms into an insufferable mutt. He yaps incessantly for so many reasons! A cat meowing in the distance, the letter carrier crossing the road, a leaf falling from a tree, a plane flying above us, me breathing—all of it makes FrouFrou go **cuckoo!**

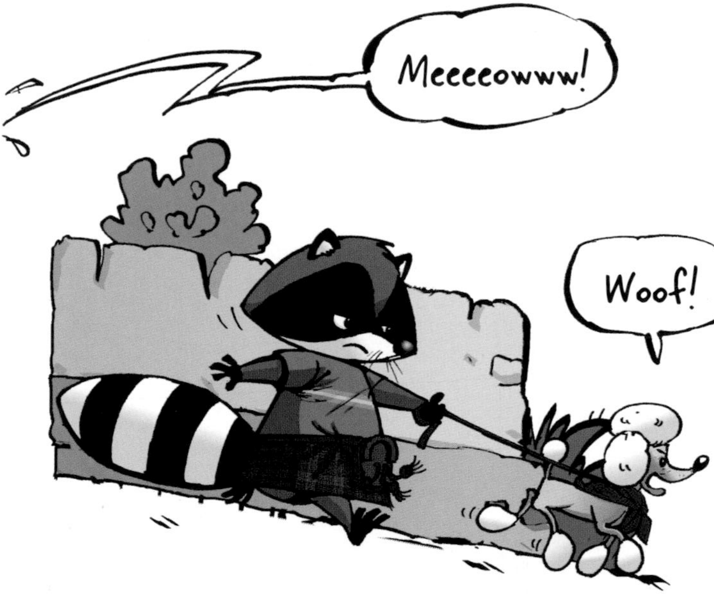
Meeeeowww!
Woof!

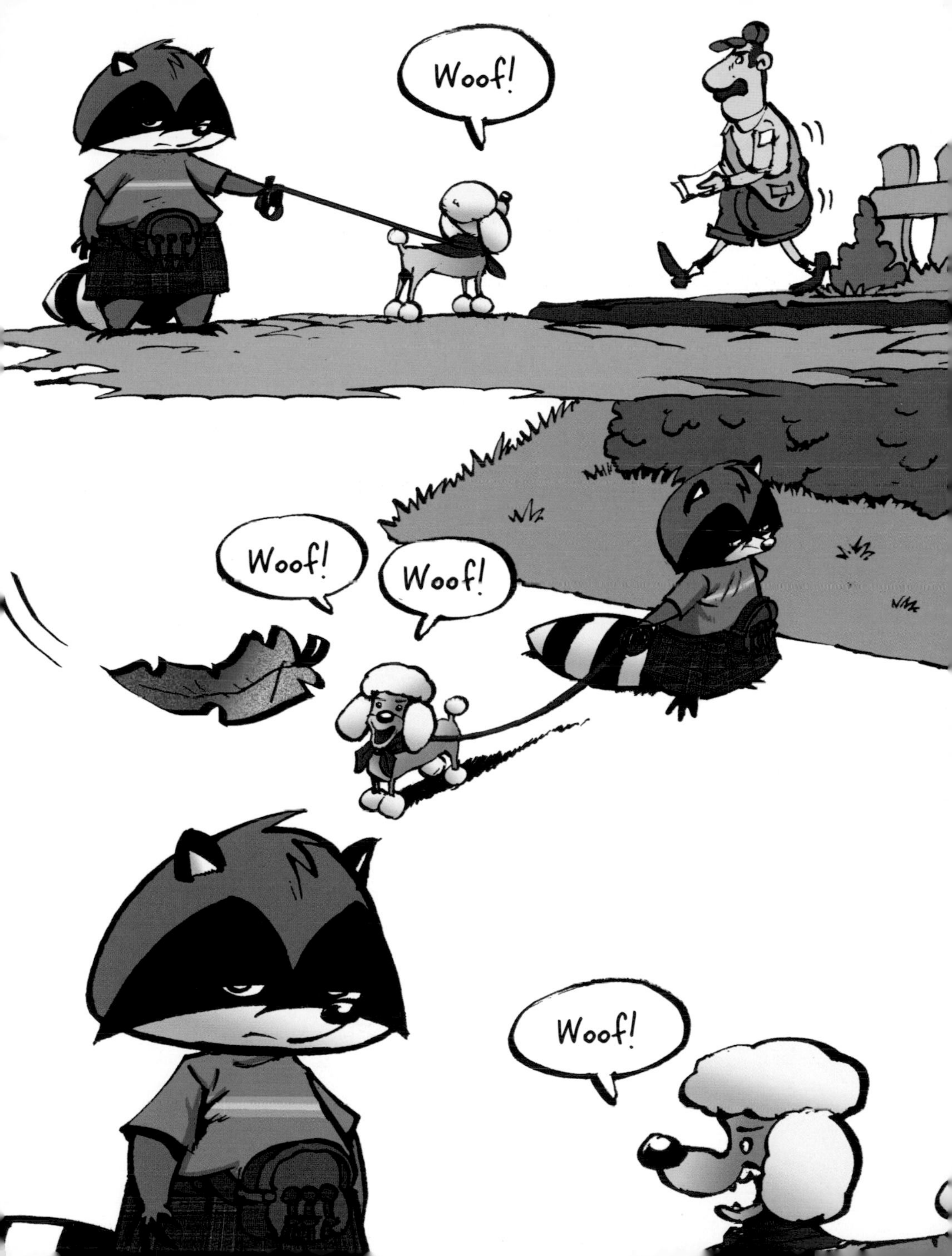
Woof!
Woof!
Woof!
Woof!

He pulls his leash so hard that he practically tears off my arm. He sniffs everywhere, following the trails of all the other neighborhood dogs. He's not shy about leaving his own mark for whoever wants to sniff it either. And I will spare you the details of his **other needs,** which I have to pick up and bring back in a baggie! **YUUUCKKK!**

Because he likes to give me a hard time, he likes to do his business not at the beginning or the end of a walk, but in the middle. You have to remember that I have to parade around with that little baggie the entire time. And the worst thing is, he doesn't go for the edges of the park. No, he prefers well-maintained lawns, especially the ones on Yellow Road. **It's the worst!!**

Of course, every time it happens it's ME that gets in trouble for where FrouFrou goes to the bathroom, like it was me who soiled the precious lawn. Me, the one who has the reputation for cleaning my food before eating it!

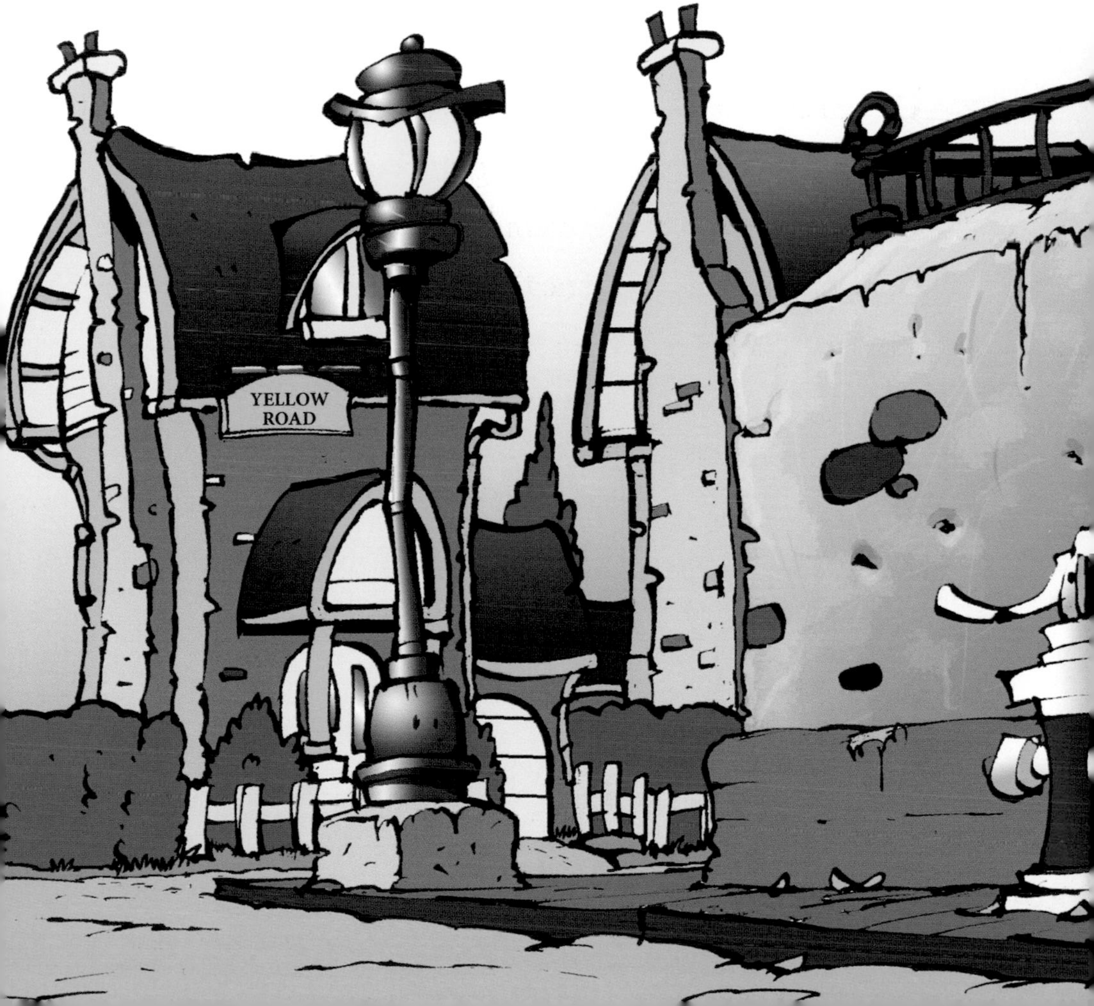
YELLOW
ROAD

I would also like very much for FrouFrou to lose his awful habit of sniffing the rear ends of unfamiliar dogs when making their acquaintance. Do I do that with the new kids at school?

It's so **embarrassing!**

I've come to really hate our daily walks.

When I talk to my parents about quitting this horrible job, they give me their standard lecture on the importance of honoring my commitments.

"The agreement with the MacTerrings ends when summer ends," my father reminds me.

I protest:

"But the end of the summer! That's a 𝔠𝔢𝔫𝔱𝔲𝔯𝔶 away!"

There is no more discussion. I am doomed to **waste** my summer holiday taking care of FrouFrou.

As soon as we are out of the line of sight of the MacTerrings, FrouFrou transforms into a giant pain. And me? I put a brown paper bag on my head.

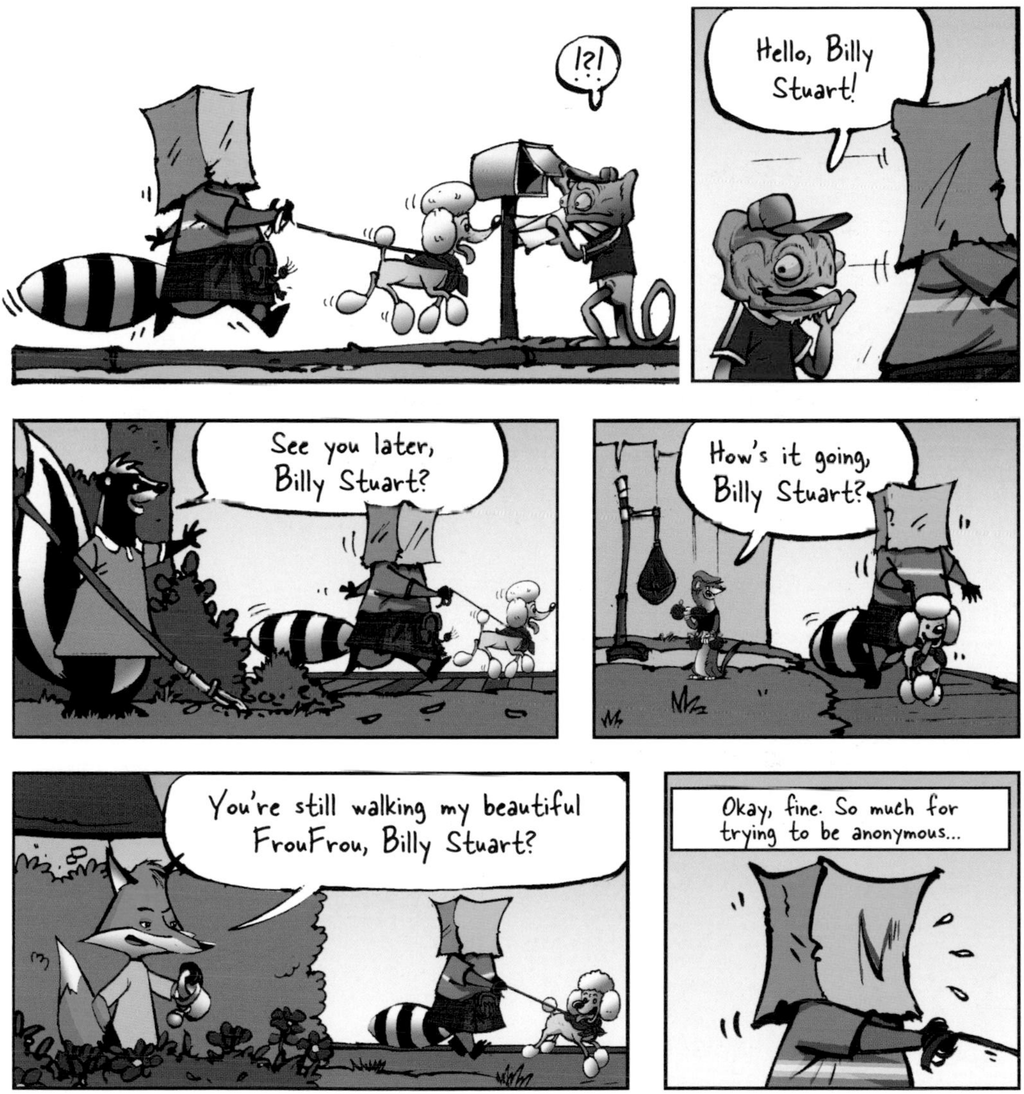
!?!
Hello, Billy Stuart!
See you later, Billy Stuart?
How's it going, Billy Stuart?
You're still walking my beautiful FrouFrou, Billy Stuart?
Okay, fine. So much for trying to be anonymous...

GET LOST!

TOWN OF CAVENDISH

One nice afternoon, after hearing FrouFrou barking in his kennel over everything and nothing at all, Billy Stuart made a decision.

"We're going to go for a long walk, you and me."

"Woof!" answered FrouFrou.

Billy put the dog in his bicycle basket and rode for fifteen minutes through the pretty town of Cavendish. He stopped and put FrouFrou down at the side of the road.

"Stay, you dirty mutt!" Billy ordered.

"Woof!" answered FrouFrou.

Satisfied, Billy headed home. When he got there, he saw FrouFrou sitting on the porch. The dog started yapping as soon as he spotted the letter carrier. Billy Stuart took FrouFrou, put him back in his bike basket and rode for twenty minutes. He stopped and put him down at the side of the road.

"Stay, you dirty mutt!" Billy ordered.

"Woof!" FrouFrou replied.

Satisfied, Billy headed home. Arriving there, he saw FrouFrou sitting on the porch. The dog started yapping at the sight of a squirrel. So Billy Stuart put FrouFrou in his basket again and rode for thirty minutes. Then he turned left.

He rode for another ten minutes before turning right, then left, then backtracking five hundred meters. He finally stopped and put the dog down by the side of the road.

"Stay, you dirty mutt!" he commanded.

"Woof!" FrouFrou responded.

A while later Billy Stuart stopped at a telephone and called his mother.

"Mom, is FrouFrou at home?"

"Yes, Billy, your dog is on the porch. He's barking at the birds."

"He's not my dog, Mom. Can I talk to him for a few minutes?"

"Why?" asked his mother.

"Because I'm loooooooost!"

Author's note
A little clarification...

To you, dear reader, I owe some explanation at this stage of the story.

First of all, let me introduce myself. I am Alain M. Bergeron, the author to whom Billy Stuart has told his many adventures.

Over the course of these pages, you will notice I feel the need to add my two cents directly into Billy's story, so as to:

- clarify a point or some bit of information;
- add a personal commentary;
- amuse myself;
- all of the above.

My presence in this book and the following ones will be through the use of an author's note. These little interruptions look like a note glued to a page.

And now, you can get back to your reading.

AM.B

Chapter 2

Enough Is Enough!

Do I look more like my FATHER or my *mother*?

My parents have different opinions on this subject. My father pretends that I am all him, his spitting image. My mother believes the opposite, that my features are all her. Personally, I think I am A HAPPY MIX OF *the two of them.*

This is a delicate subject in the Stuart family. I already asked this question of Mrs. and Mr. Stuart. Billy is right—he looks as much like his mother as his father.

As for my character, once again my parents **disagree**. It's on a case-by-case basis. When I have completed a very complicated task—for example, tied a good knot in a scarf, which not just anybody can do—my mother and my father rave about my abilities.

"That definitely comes from *my* side of the family!" each one argues.

But if I mess up—say, I break a window playing ball with my friends—they make it the other one's fault.

"That's definitely from *your* side of the family."

But me, Billy Stuart, I'm the kind of raccoon who knows how to compromise. I have my father's gutsy temperament *and* my mother's intelligence.

I am also naturally very curious. This is part of the reason why I joined the **SCOUTS**.

I rapidly climbed the ranks of the Zintrepids pack. And due to certain circumstances and my **ability** to knot scarves—and friendships—I became the leader. Okay, so there's not many in our troop (five, including me), but it's a start. Other members may still join us.

I follow in my paternal grandfather's **footsteps**. I have inherited his love of fresh air and his taste for ***ADVENTURE***. His name is Virgil Stuart. I adore him. If I could, I would cross raging rapids, I would hike mountains with the highest peaks, I would brave the worst **DANGERS** with him.

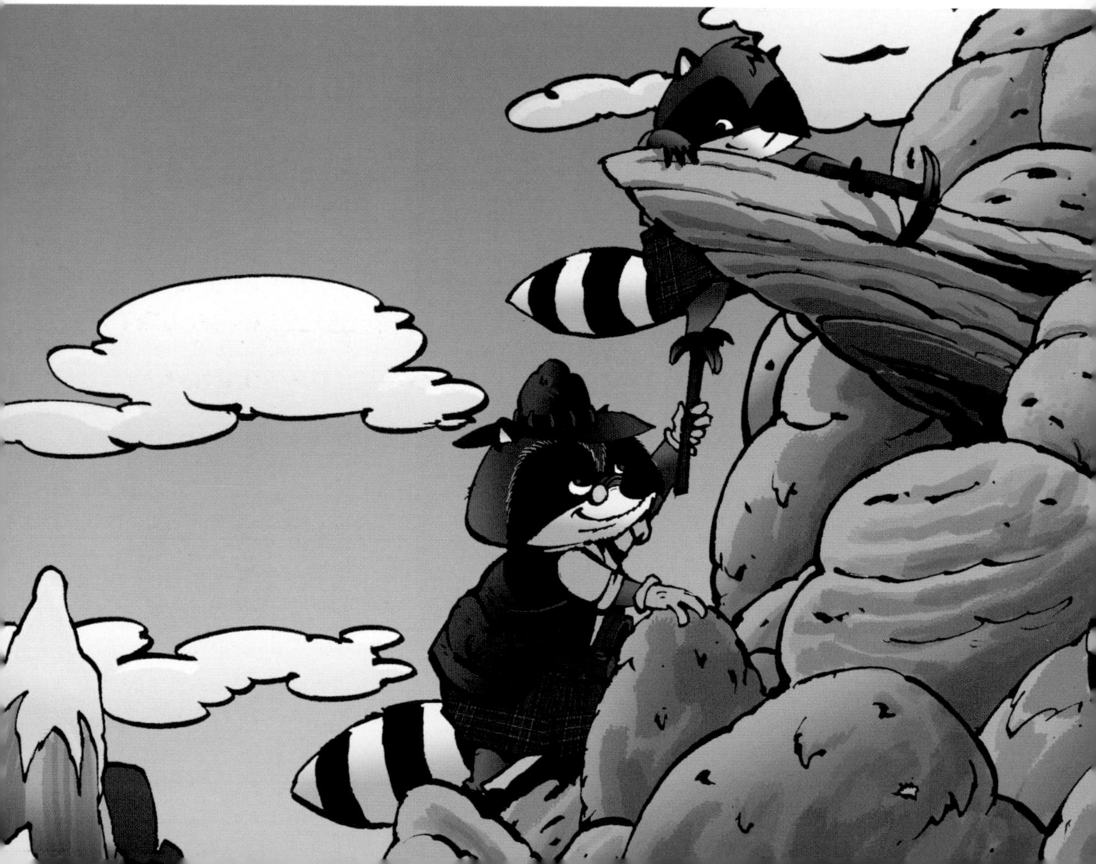

There is no corner of this round planet that he hasn't explored. The world holds no more secrets for this great voyager. One day I would love for him to take me along in his luggage so I could escape my *daily grind*. All the stories he could tell me…

Yup! After thinking about it, he's who I want to be like.

Note to Billy Stuart's parents: Please don't be offended.

But today I would prefer to be invisible, like a puff of wind!

My dad and my mom want to help my neighbors out of a fix. The MacTerrings will be going on **holiday** in Europe for a month. The Zazou team, the boarding kennel to which they entrust FrouFrou, has closed its doors for the summer.

There the MacTerrings are, the two of them, on our doorstep, looking bashful.

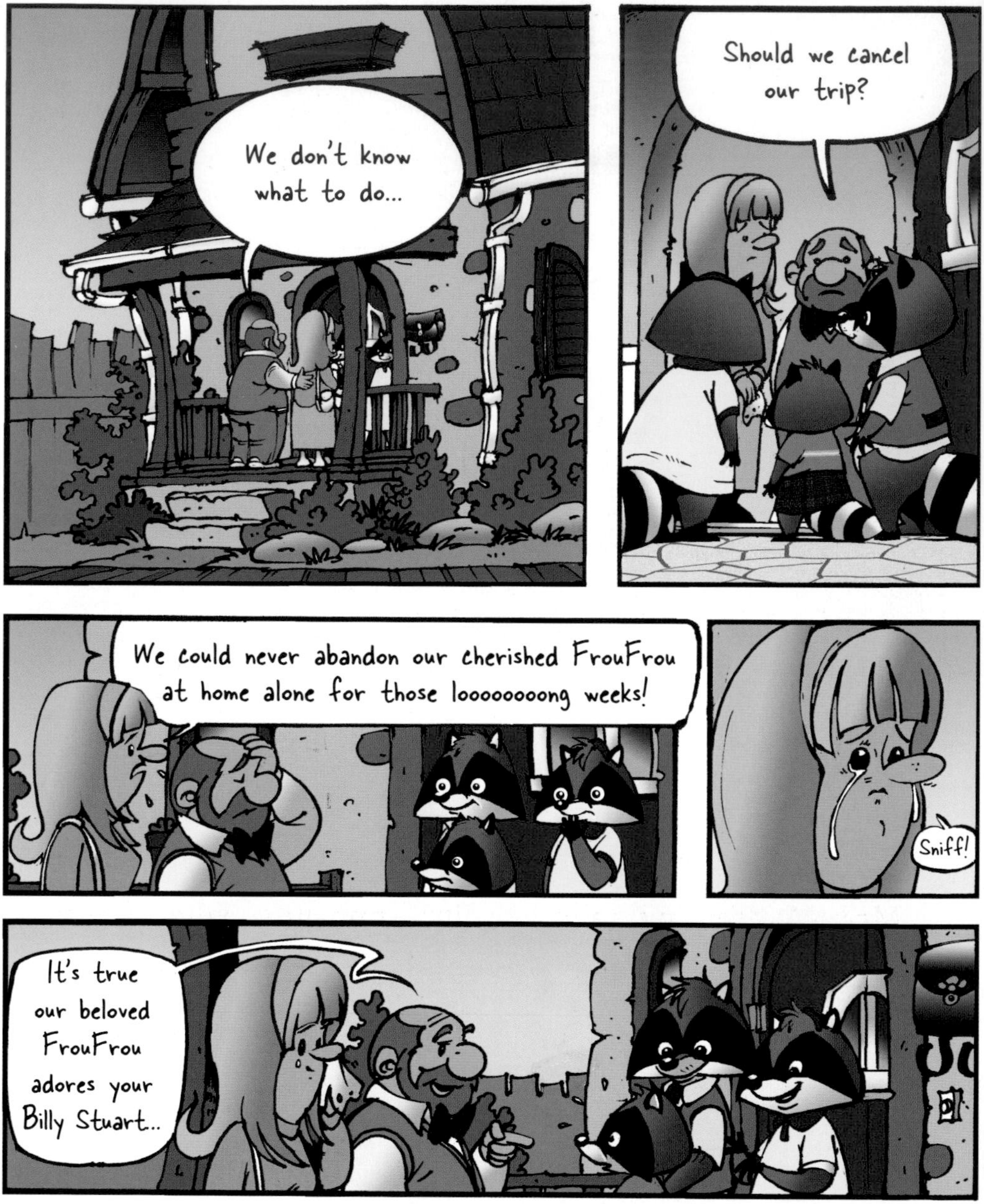
We don't know what to do...
Should we cancel our trip?
We could never abandon our cherished FrouFrou at home alone for those looooooong weeks!
Sniff!
It's true our beloved FrouFrou adores your Billy Stuart...

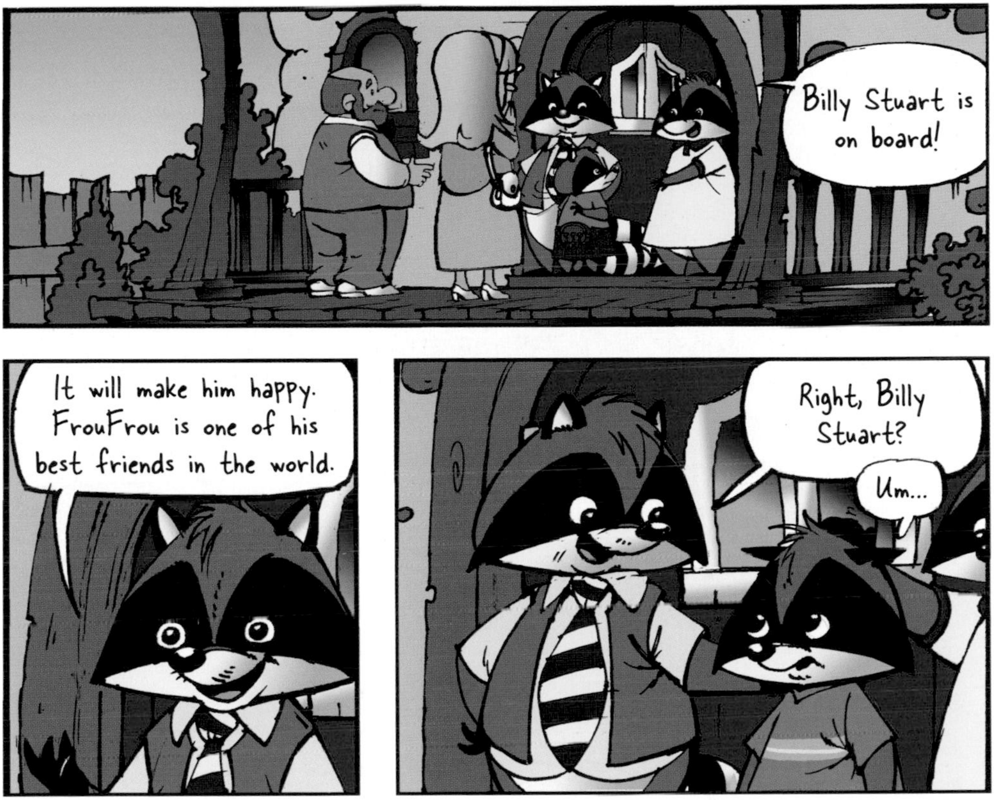
Billy Stuart is on board!
It will make him happy. FrouFrou is one of his best friends in the world.
Right, Billy Stuart?
Um...

The MacTerrings take this as a yes. They rejoice. Mrs. MacTerring calls her little pup-pup, who comes bounding over. He jumps on me, knocking me to the ground. That dirty dog licks my face! YUCK! His breath smells like dog, that beast! When I think of what else he's cleaned with that tongue? DIS-GUS-TING!

Our neighbors waste no time! They return with their arms full. They have food, a blue blanket, a plastic toy that goes **put–put** when you press it and makes the pooch go crazy, a cushion and a box of biscuits that, should you make the **mistake** of shaking it, causes another round of excitement. All this stuff just for the dog's sense of well-being?!?

The MacTerrings give my parents an instruction list with a schedule of naps, meals and exercises.

"FrouFrou doesn't like sleeping alone," says Mrs. MacTerring. "If he doesn't know you are at his side, he could bark all night long."

WHAT? I have to share my room with this nightmare of a dog?

Mr. MacTerring gives my mother some earplugs.

"They're for Billy Stuart," he tells her, "because FrouFrou snores like a lawn mower..."

HEEEEEELP!

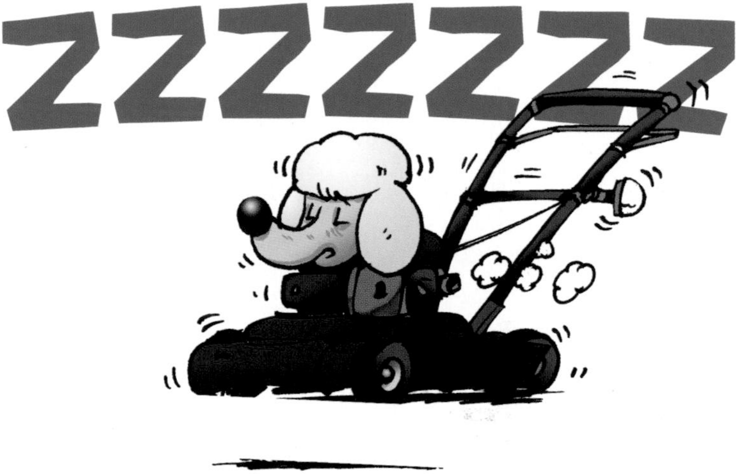
ZZZZZZZ

Chapter 3

A Letter from My Grandfather

It's not true that the dog snores like a lawn mower. He snores like an airplane engine! And the earplugs do **absolutely nothing!** I have to keep my bedroom window closed. Otherwise all my neighbors on Red Tartan Road would get woken up. **And guess who would be blamed?**

> I live a couple of streets over from Billy Stuart, in the gray-house area, and I can verify that on certain nights, when the wind blows eastward, it brings with it a deafening hum.

He snores all NIGHT and barks all day. He is a walking testament to noise on four paws.

And it will be like this until the end of my holidays. I can't wait to get back to school!

I am busy thinking about 1,001 ways to get rid of him as I throw a tennis ball against the wall. The dog grabs it each time and brings it back to me. I keep this game up for several minutes. Useless to think FrouFrou will give up. The wall will cave in before this dog runs out of energy.

It's my mom who catches the ball with her hand this time.

"Bravo! Way to go, Mom! Bring back the ball!"

She **laughs**.

"Why is the ball is wet? Did it fall in a puddle?"

"No, it's that **SLOBBERING** dog."

Her sense of humor disappears. From her pocket she takes out an envelope and passes it to me.

FrouFrou twirls around her, springing up on his hind legs.

"The ball, Mom!" I tell her, ripping open the letter.

Fantastic! A letter from my grandfather.

My mother throws the ball down the hallway.

The dog, excited, tries to take off but can't get moving. His claws have no traction on the wood floor. You'd think he was tap-dancing.

Infuriated by the scratches on her wood floor, my mom screams just as the dog finally manages to take off.

"It's not me!" I cut my toenails every week.

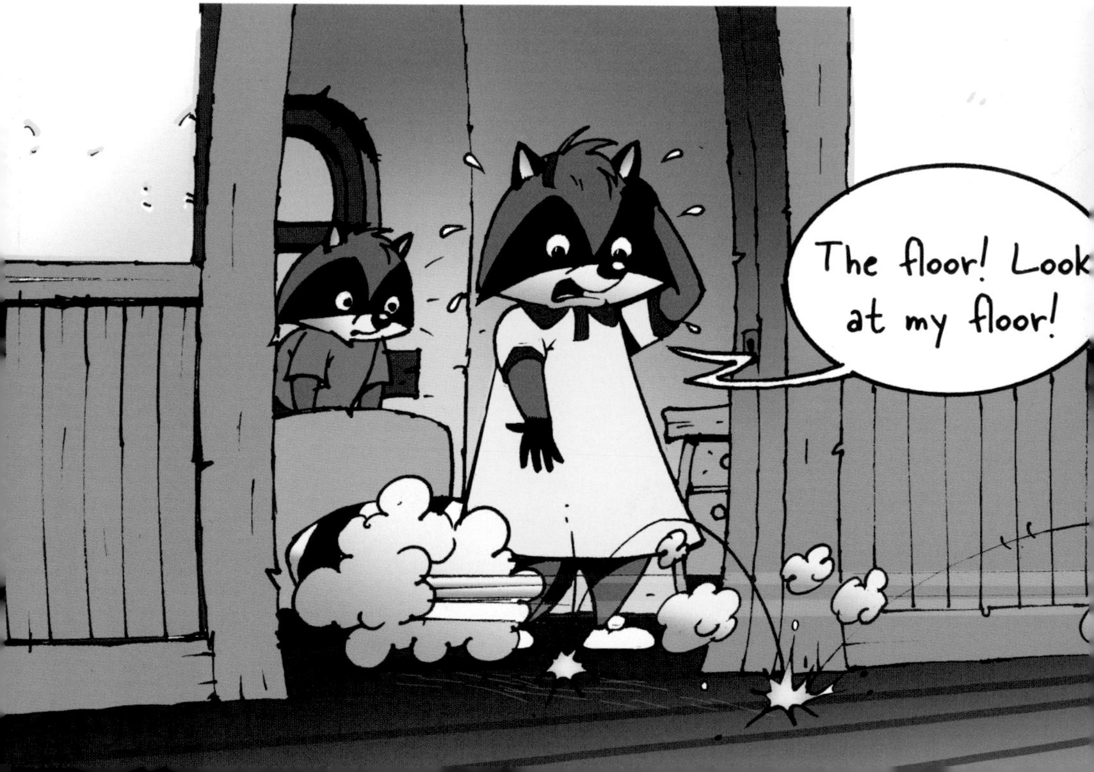
The floor! Look at my floor!

The ball bounds down the hallway and…

CRASH!!!

By the sound of it, I'd say that was the porcelain thingamajig on the little table.

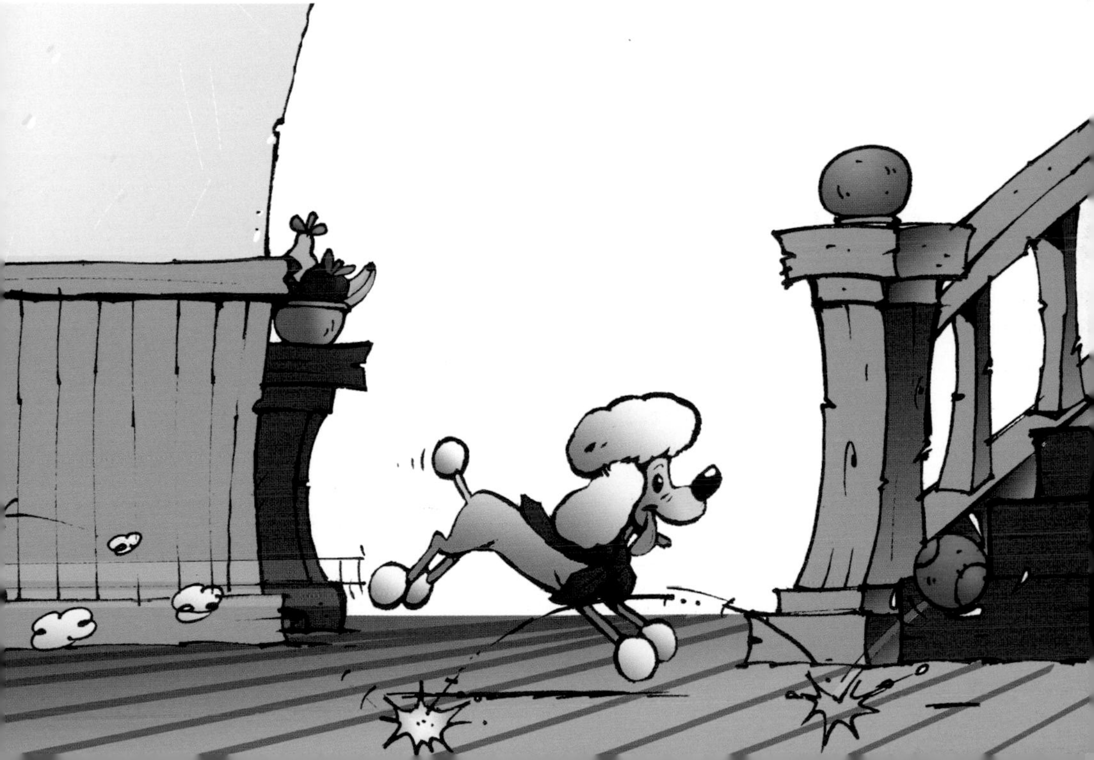

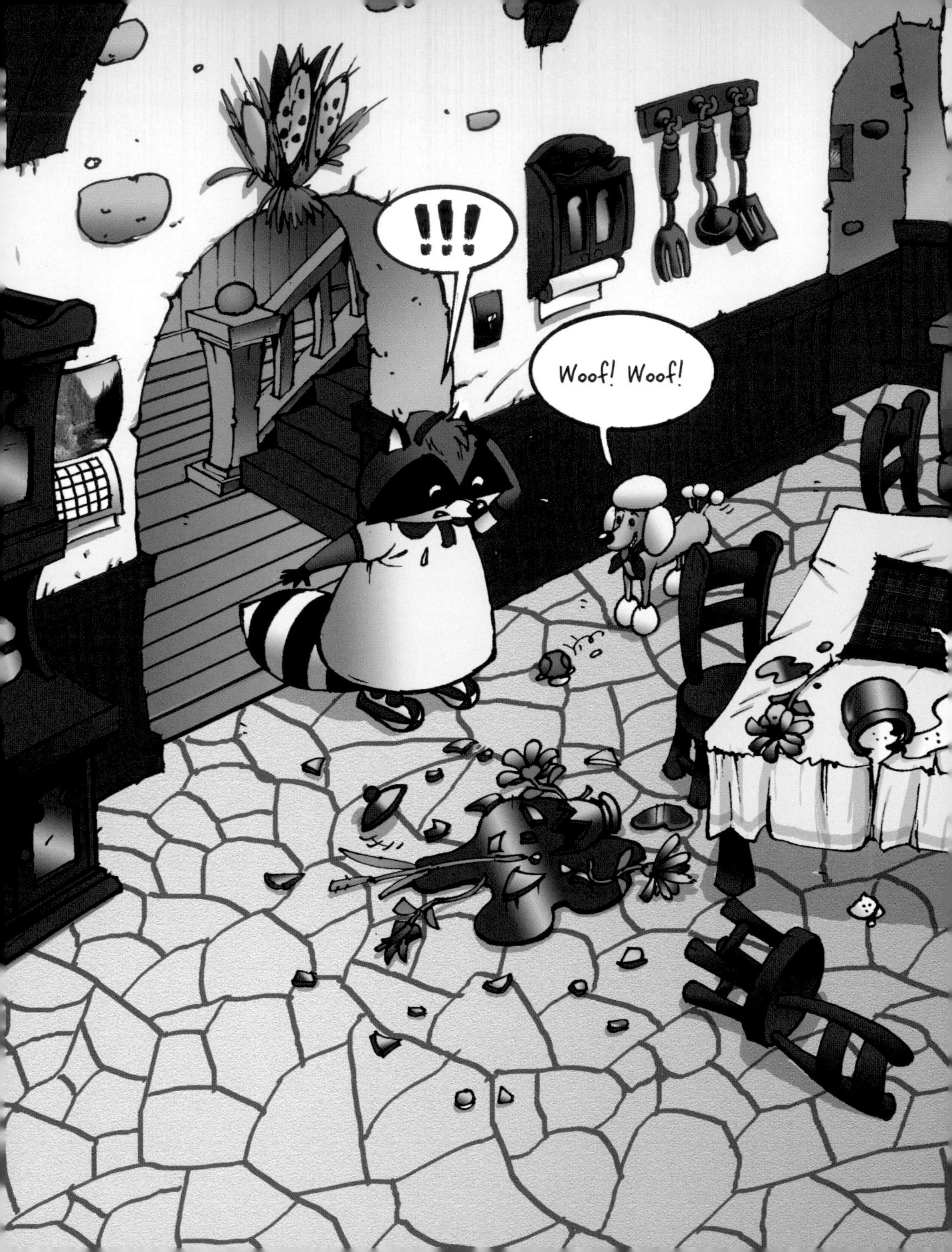
!!!
Woof! Woof!

B O O M !

And that noise there? That's FrouFrou, who collides with the table because the floor is **slippery** in that spot.

My mom inspects the damage. She yells at the dog, who is yapping with **delight,** hoping the game will continue.

I take advantage of her distraction to sneak off to my room to read my grandfather Virgil's letter.

I have a photocopy of the famous letter. In lots of places, it's pretty illegible. Like a doctor's hurried handwriting on a prescription. Still, Billy Stuart had no trouble reading it. I will show it to you in two forms, handwritten and transcribed on a computer.

Cavendish, July 13

My dear Billy Stuart,

Today I made a sensational discovery. You know I've always believed in time travel. Not with a machine like H. G. Wells's—that's pretend—but through passageways.

It's like the Earth keeps a door open to its history. Fascinating, right? These passageways have been traveled for centuries by insiders.

Now I have found one of these passageways. Yes, Billy Stuart! It is located in Belcher's Cavern, near the fork in the Bulstrode River, in the heart of Kanuks Forest. I have no idea where it will take me, but I must follow this passage. This will be the most important adventure of my life!

Come join me tomorrow, around two o'clock, to see me off on my big adventure.

I am so looking forward to seeing you—and to going!

Your favorite grandfather,

Virgil Stuart

P.S. Say nothing to your parents. They would only worry about me.

Cavendish, July 13

My dear Billy Stuart,

Today I made a sensational discovery. You know I've always believed in time travel. Not with a machine like H.G. Wells's—that's pretend—but through passageways.

It's like the Earth keeps a door open to its history. Fascinating, right? These passageways have been traveled for centuries by insiders.

Now I have found one of these passageways. Yes, Billy Stuart! It is located in Belcher's Cavern, near the fork in the Bulstrode River, in the heart of Kanuks Forest. I have no idea where it will take me, but I must follow this passage. This will be the most important adventure of my life!

Come join me tomorrow, around two o'clock, to see me off on my big adventure.

I am so looking forward to seeing you—and to going!

Your favorite grandfather,

Virgil Stuart

P.S. Say nothing to your parents. They would only worry about me.

KABILLIONS of crusty-clawed crawfish in that Bulstrode River!

My grandfather is actually going to time-travel!

I am **shocked**.

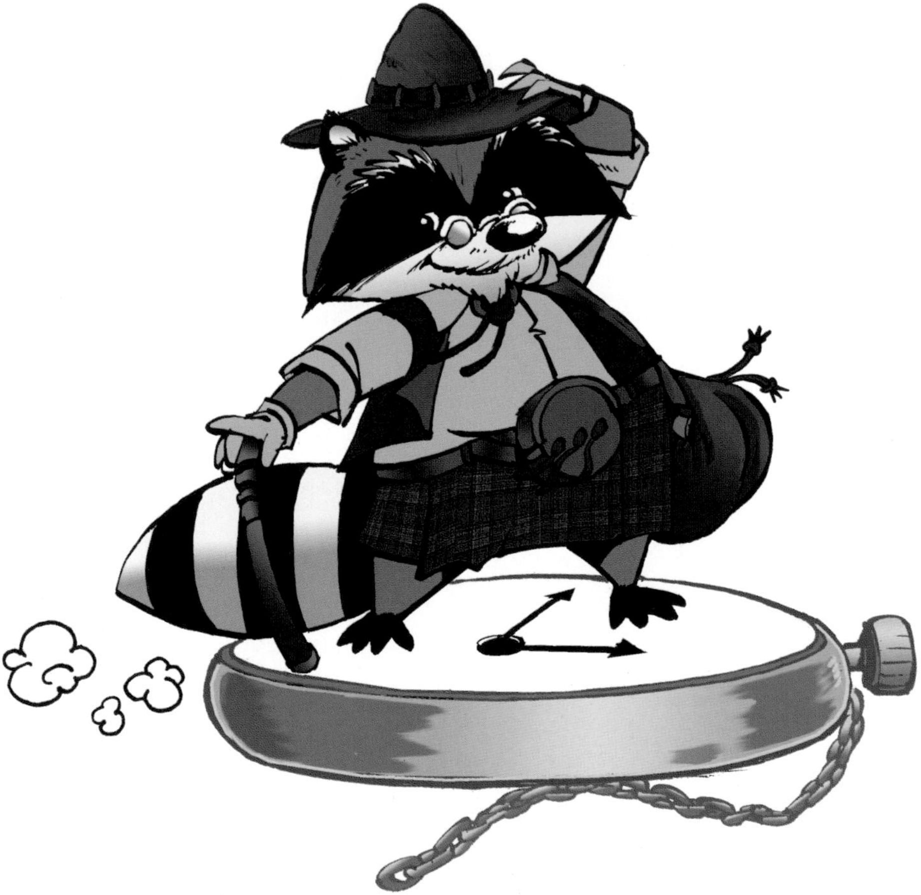

When Tomorrow Is Today

It's fantastic!

My grandfather Virgil has discovered a way to travel through time, and he has invited me to come see him before he leaves! How I would like to go back in time a few days to the very moment I offered to walk the MacTerrings' dog! I would go instead to Foxy, the fox, who adooooooooores FrouFrou, and suggest that she look after the poodle. I would make *her* walk FrouFrou—and I would be enjoying my dream summer vacation!

I wonder how my grandfather has mastered the art of time travel. How is he able to determine where he'll end up? And where has he decided to go? To the dinosaur age maybe? And what if I suggest FrouFrou go with him? And what if a TYRANNOSAURUS puts him on his menu? The dog, not my grandfather!

One can dream…

I reread Grandpa's letter. Something feels odd, but I can't figure out what.

His jerky handwriting, indecipherable to common mortals? No, it isn't that. His signature? Not that either. I recognize his Y, made up of two lines that extend past the base, giving the impression that the Y is an X.

My eyes focus on the date.

Suddenly it's obvious. July 13!

KABILLIONS of crusty-clawed crawfish in that Bulstrode River!

The thirteenth of July was yesterday!

I skim the letter one more time.

Come join me tomorrow…

My brain is **REELING**. Tomorrow, for my grandfather, was July 14! And the fourteenth of July, for me, is TODAY! We are on his tomorrow, and he's scheduled the meeting for

…around two o'clock…

In one hour!

I am just about to leave my room when I spot my folded uniform on the back of my chair.

On the fourteenth of July at two o'clock, I already have a meeting!

The Zintrepids have a forest hike planned for that time! You'd think I wouldn't forget a meeting on the fourteenth day of the month at fourteen hundred hours—what two o'clock is for those of you who aren't Scouts.

My mind works with great Velocity with a capital *V*, for Virgil. Where is the meet-up spot for the troop going to be? At the start of the Bulstrode River trail.

We must: go partway up the river, make a fishing rod with whatever we can find on the banks, catch fish, clean them, make a fire and cook our dinners and, the ultimate test, eat our catch.

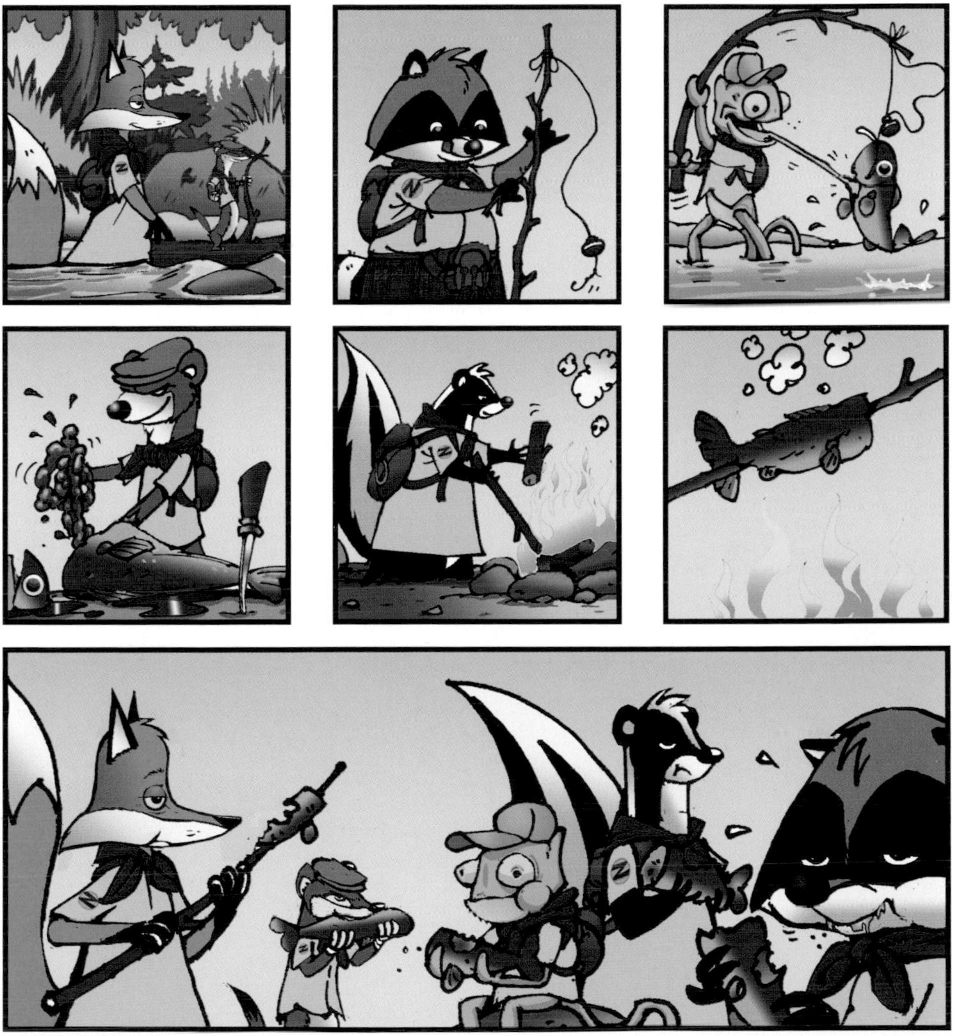

If we fail, we can always count on the canned tuna that Foxy will undoubtedly bring. Yuck!

Even thinking about it makes me nauseated. I would prefer a crawfish pizza.

If I have correctly deciphered the map of the terrain, we won't be far from the cavern that my grandfather mentioned. If I **hurry**, I will make it. Wouldn't it be funny to be late to see someone off on their time-traveling expedition?

I adjust my kilt and put on my uniform in a few swift movements. My nimble fingers knot the scarf around my neck.

FrouFrou is fast on my heels the minute I set foot outside my room. Near the front door, with my index finger pointed menacingly at him, I order, "STAY! Billy Stuart—that's me, dirty mutt!—will be back soon."

As if the dog can understand the nature of *soon*. If I'd said **in a hundred years**, it would have made no difference.

DO YOU KNOW YOUR COLORS?

SAY OUT LOUD WHAT COLOR
THESE WORDS ARE:

RED	GREEN	RED
BLUE	BLUE	BLUE
GREEN	BLUE	
RED	BLUE	
GREEN	RED	
GREEN	BLUE	
RED	BLUE	
GREEN	GREEN	

The moment I open the door to run, my mother stops me.

"Where are you going, young raccoon?"

"**Um**...the Zintrepids."

I can't waste a precious second explaining everything to her, especially not the story about my grandfather. My reply isn't lying, and I'm not worrying her.

Anxiously I glance at the hallway clock. I stomp up and down on the spot like I have to go to the toilet and it's occupied.

"Okay. Enjoy yourself," says my mother. "**Be** careful. **Watch** out for black bears. Storms are forecast for this afternoon. Do you have your raincoat? Don't **speak** to strangers. **Avoid**—"

"Thanks, Mom! Bye!"

I am almost outside when I hear her shout, "**ONE MINUTE!** And this?"

I knew it! You can guess what *this* is. *This* is that gem of a dog, panting in anticipation, leaping for joy on his hind legs because he thinks it's time for his daily walk.

"What, this?"

"**THIS**," she says, "is **YOUR** responsibility. You can't leave FrouFrou all alone. He will miss you so much, he will **DESTROY** your room before you get back."

My mother takes down the leash from the hallway cupboard and attaches it to FrouFrou's collar.

"He can come with you. A little **exercise** will do him a world of good."

Normally I listen to my parents without grumbling. But there is no way I am bringing FrouFrou to the FOREST. So I decide to argue with my mother.

"No! I don't want to! He can just wait here. He annoys my friends," I tell her. I stand firm, arms crossed against my chest.

There! That wasn't as hard as I'd feared. All you have to do is assert yourself…

Chapter 5

The Zintrepids' Anthem

"Stay still!"

The leash is strained to its full length. FrouFrou is ahead of me on the narrow path that leads to the trail near the Bulstrode River. He is *pulling* and is practically strangling himself.

"Heel!"

My command yields no effect. I could just as well be shouting, "PIZZA!"

As soon as the dog catches sight of my friends, he starts barking. When he hears Foxy calling him, he can't contain himself.

"Come see me, my beautiful FrouFrou! *Sweetie pie,* how I love you, how I *adore* you!"

The poodle's tail wags like a metronome. Panting, he strains at the end of his leash, standing on his hind legs, his upper body pulled forward, front feet pedaling in the air. He is going to dislocate my shoulder! **Okay, okay**—I free him.

Off leash, the animal gallops toward Foxy's open arms. Their reunion drips with drool. **YUCK!**

FrouFrou licks the fox's face, who doesn't shy away from this canine affection. Too bad for you, Foxy! **HA! HA! HA!**

My friend knows I can't stand the dog, which for her is a reason to love him even more. The other members of the pack don't agree.

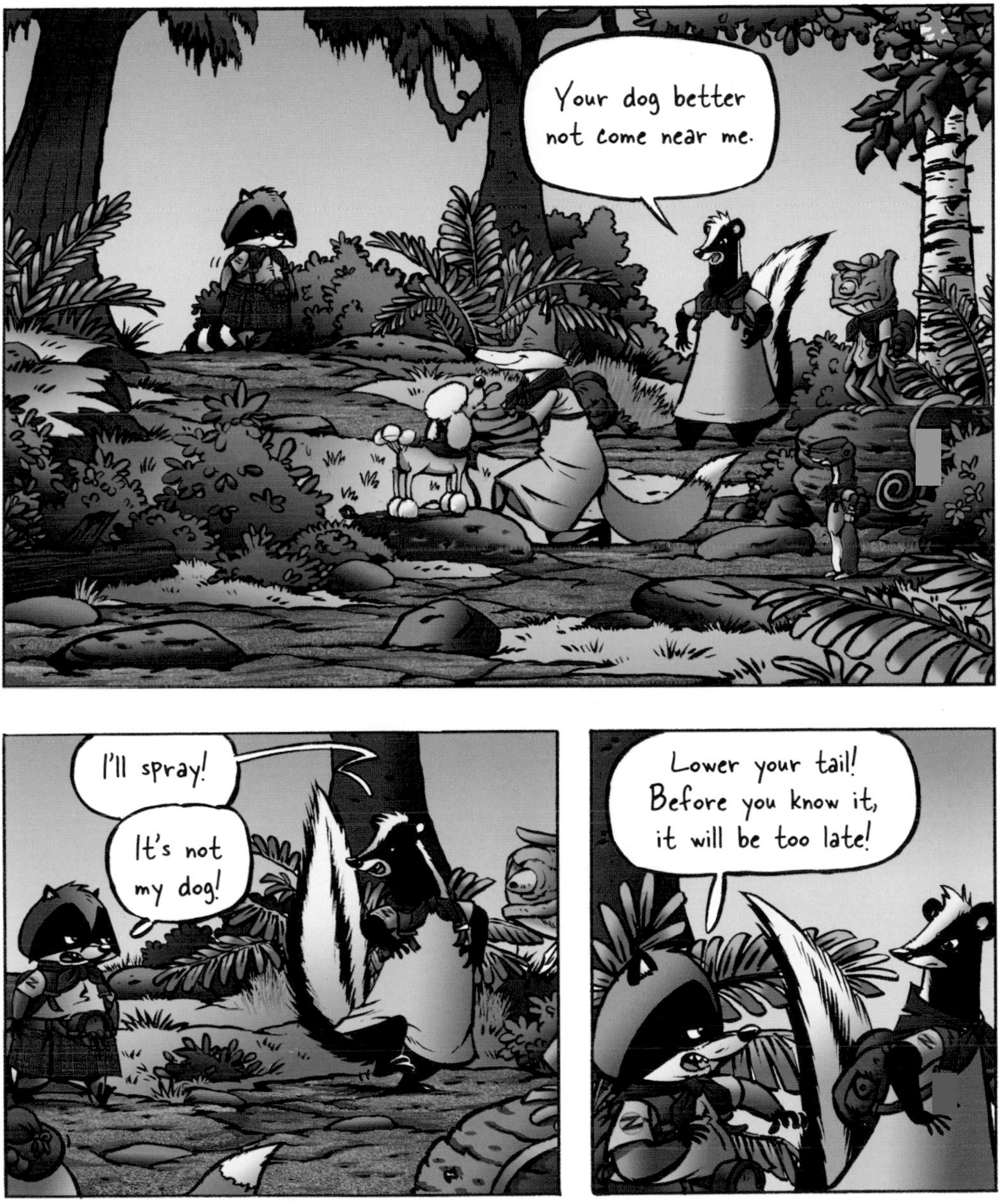
Your dog better not come near me.
I'll spray!
It's not my dog!
Lower your tail! Before you know it, it will be too late!

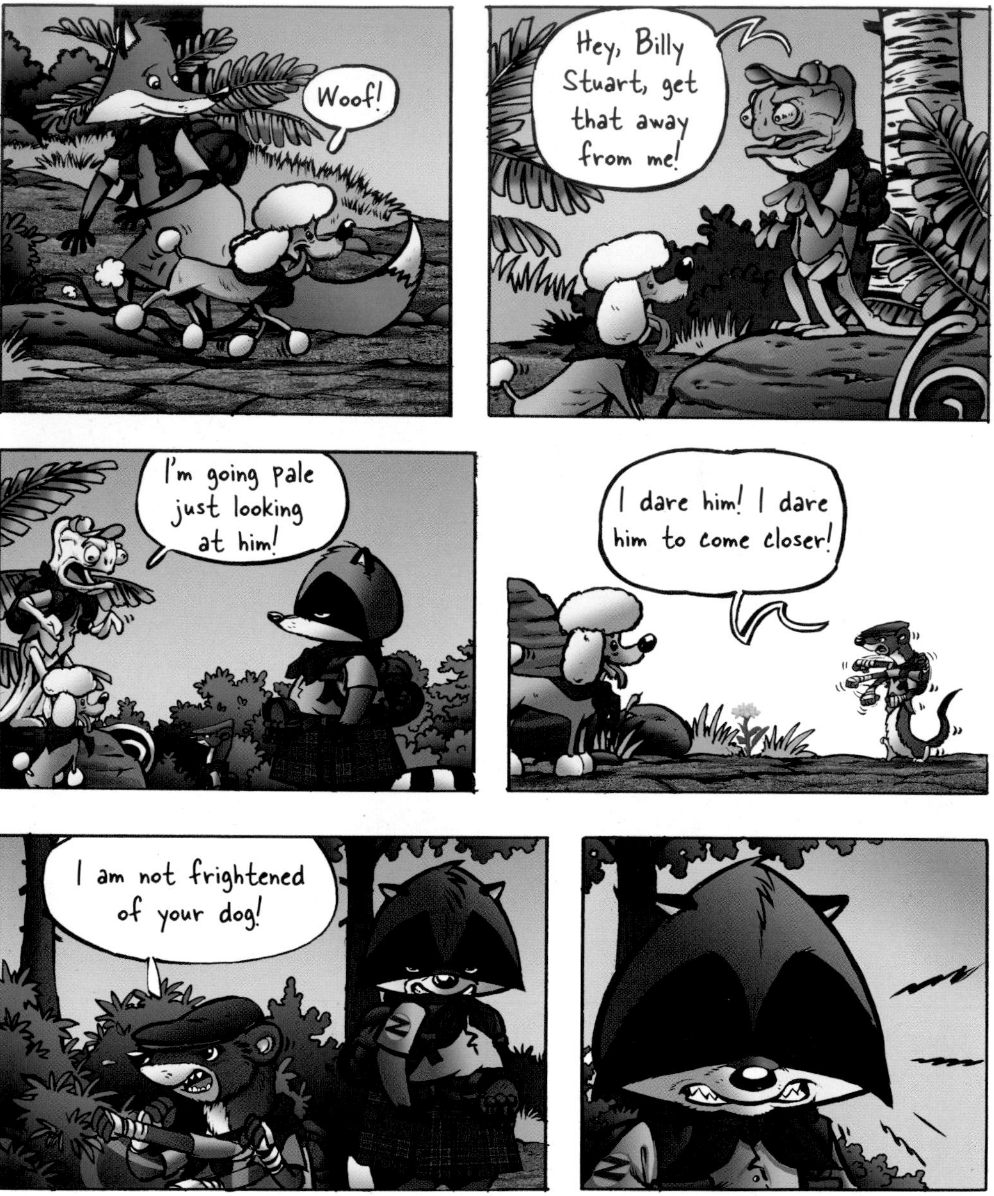
Woof!
Hey, Billy Stuart, get that away from me!
I'm going pale just looking at him!
I dare him! I dare him to come closer!
I am not frightened of your dog!

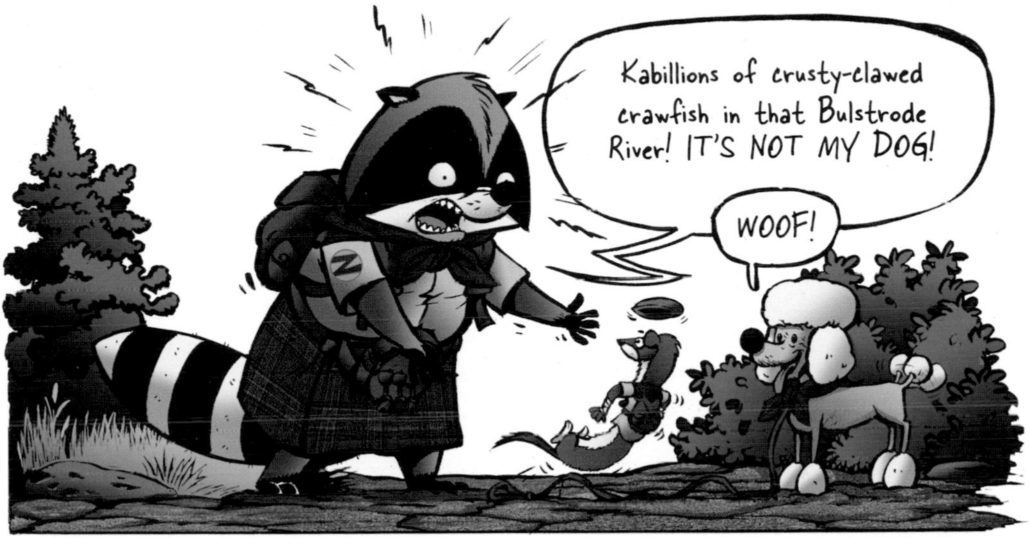
Kabillions of crusty-clawed crawfish in that Bulstrode River! IT'S NOT MY DOG!
WOOF!

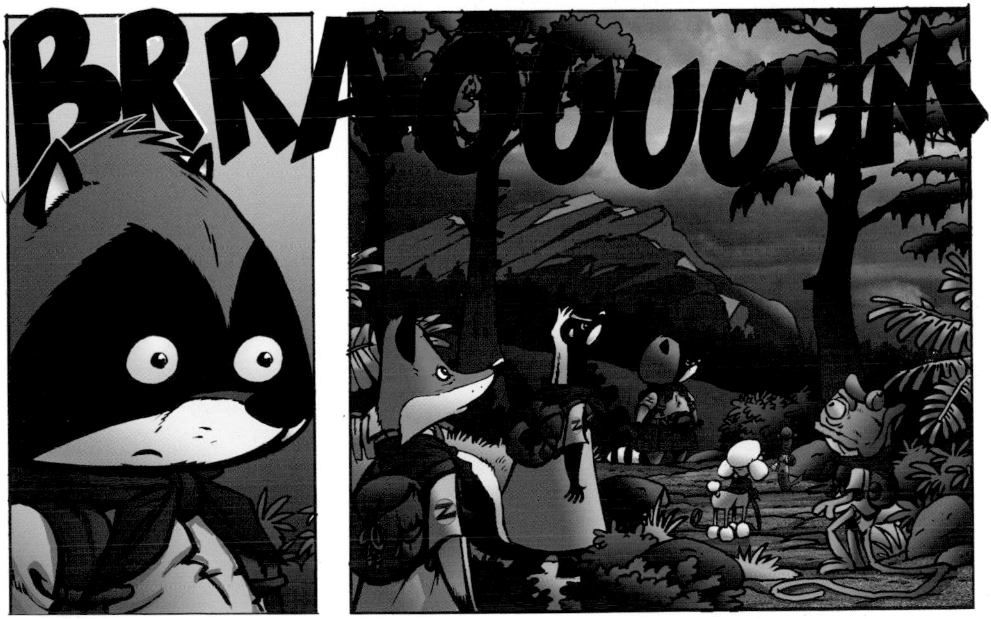
BRRAOUUUGM

TIC TOC

I will have to hurry if I want to get to Belcher's Cavern in time to meet up with my grandfather. Because I only plan on popping by for a few seconds to say hello to him, I don't think I need to explain everything to my fellow scouts. I just have to trust this wretched FrouFrou to Foxy, who really would like nothing better than to take care of him.

Although he's distracted by the smells of nature, the dog walks obediently along the trail at Foxy's side. How does she manage to keep him quietly at her side? I'll need to put my ego aside and ask her to share her trick.

I sing a song, not for fun but to signal our presence and protect us from a possible attack by BLACK BEARS.

I sing the lyrics of the Zintrepids' anthem **LOUDLY** in an exaggerated way.

We are all marching toward adventure, proud and strong...

A long time ago I heard some similar lyrics on TV. They were from a song in a cartoon called Rocket Robin Hood. Even after all these years, I can hear it in my head. Could this song have inspired the Zintrepids' anthem? Who knows?

From my very first notes, FrouFrou **HOWLS** like a **WOOOOOLF**, imitating the pack.

Suddenly a nauseating odor is in the air.

"It stinks!" Shifty complains.

Obviously, everyone turns toward Musky. But when it comes to bad smells, that skunk is overly sensitive. You could say her nose gets out of joint easily. Especially when she is accused of something she didn't do.

"You could have held it in!" Foxy scolds.

Musky is outraged to be thought of as the **cause** of this stink.

"As soon as there is the slightest bad smell, it's the skunk's fault! Go ahead! **Blame me!**"

But this time it really *doesn't* smell like Musky. Nothing compares to the stink she can release.

This smells more like outdoor toilets!

At the edge of the trail that follows the Bulstrode River, a black bear appears.

Beware the Grouchy Bear

What a furry surprise! It sure isn't Winnie-the-Pooh!

Our feet are GLUED to the ground. We absolutely must not panic. Under no circumstances can we show the beast that it is **TERRIFYING** us.

Shifty, the chameleon, transforms too quickly from black to white. Half of his body matches the bear. His other half matches the dog. What a predicament! Black or white. Ebony or ivory—like the notes of a piano.

The bear **GROWLS** and stands up on its hind legs. Upright it's huge. Its roar is terrifying.

GRRRRRRROOOOOOOOWWWL !

And then a familiar stink fills the air. This time there is no doubt where it came from!

Did you know that the bear who inspired Winnie-the-Pooh was a black bear? Her name was Winnipeg, and she belonged to a Canadian soldier, and veterinarian, named Harry Colebourn. Sent to the frontlines in France in 1915 during the First World War, he donated the bear to the London Zoo. It was there, a few years later, that a Canadian journalist who was visiting the zoo with his son saw him. This man was A.A. Milne, his son named his own stuffed bear after Winnie, and A.A. Milne was inspired to create the character of Winnie-the-Pooh. His book *Winnie-the-Pooh* was first published in 1926 with illustrations by Ernest Shepard—not Walt Disney. It was a huge success.

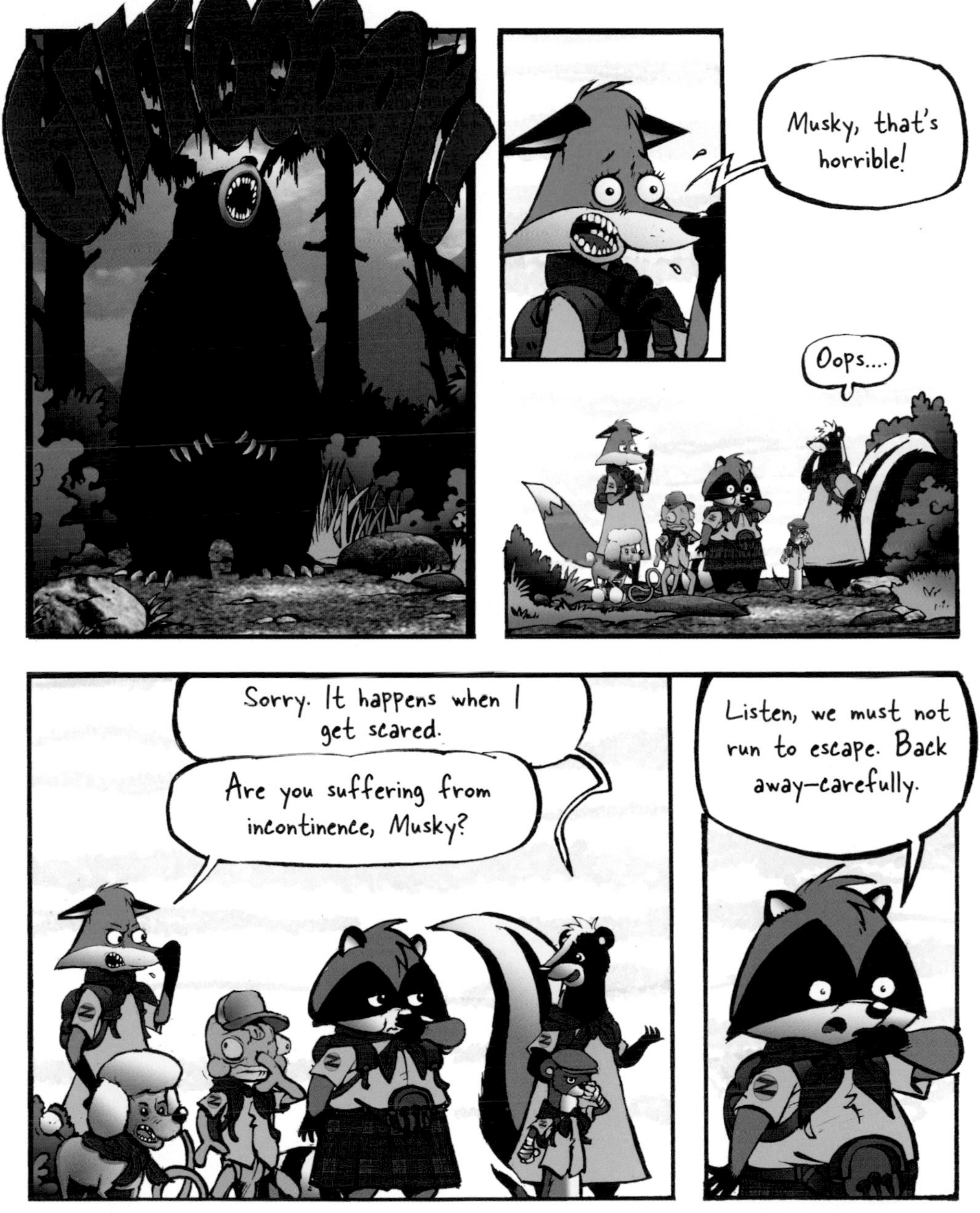
Musky, that's horrible!
Oops....
Sorry. It happens when I get scared.
Are you suffering from incontinence, Musky?
Listen, we must not run to escape. Back away—carefully.

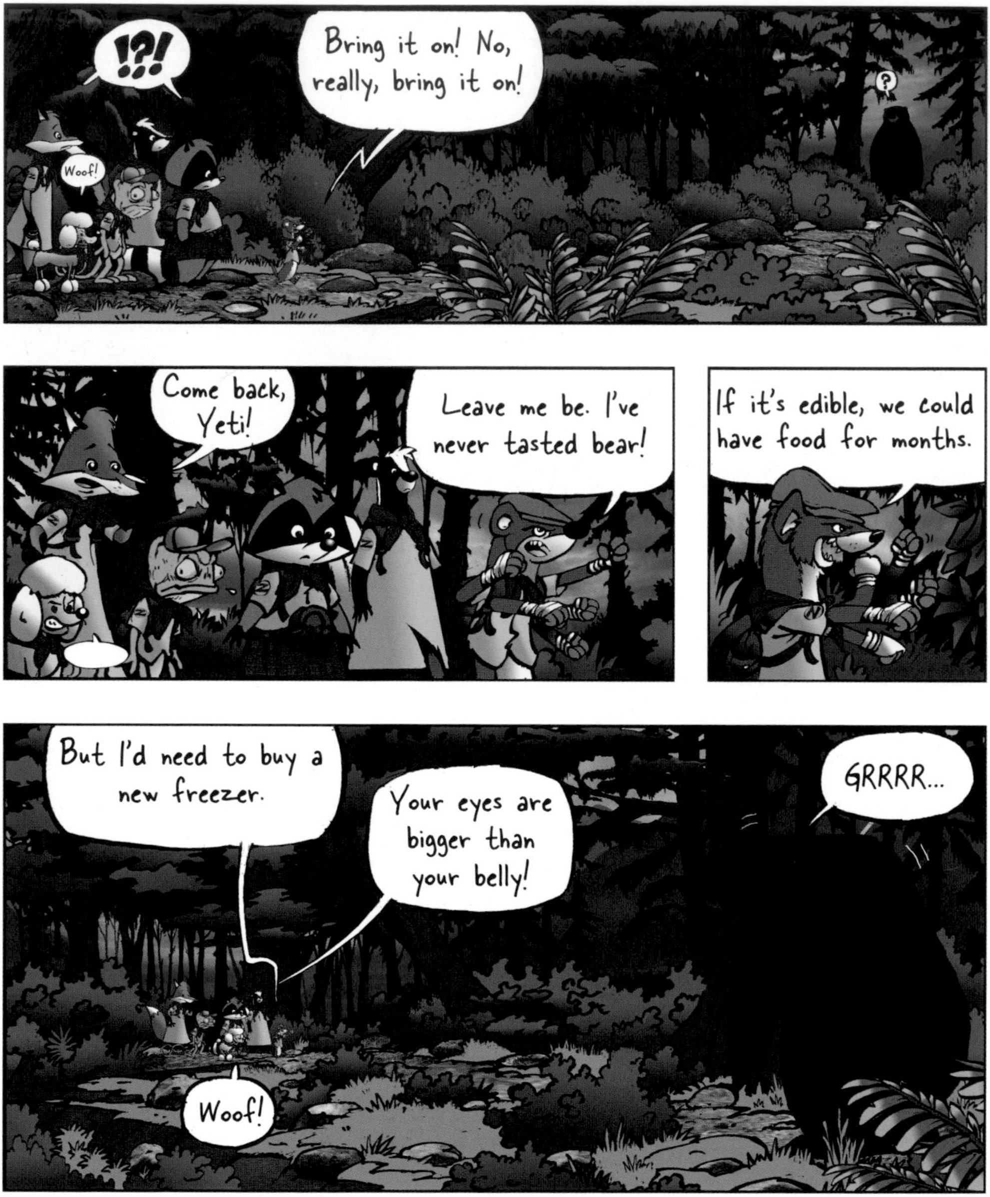
!?!
Woof!
Bring it on! No, really, bring it on!
?
Come back, Yeti!
Leave me be. I've never tasted bear!
If it's edible, we could have food for months.
But I'd need to buy a new freezer.
Your eyes are bigger than your belly!
Woof!
GRRRR...

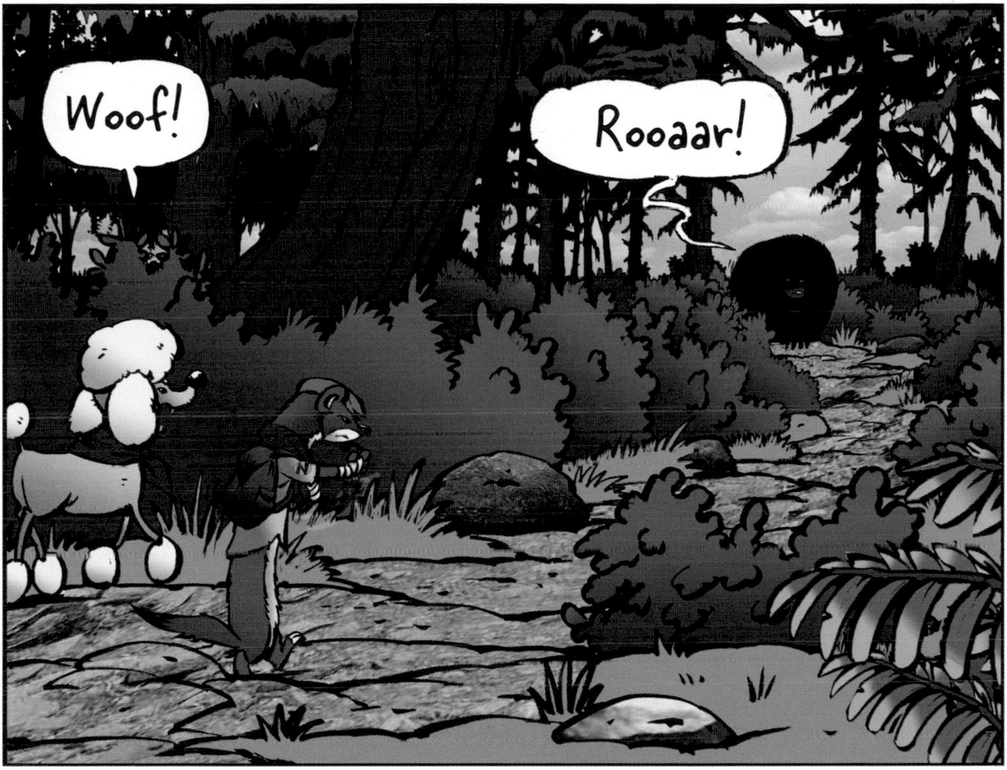
Woof!
Rooaar!

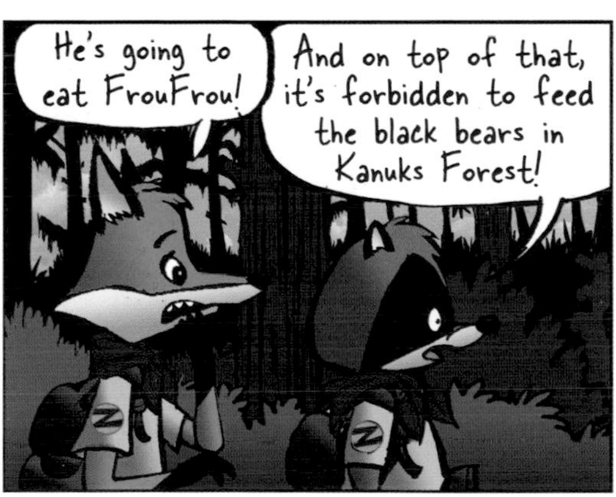
He's going to eat FrouFrou!
And on top of that, it's forbidden to feed the black bears in Kanuks Forest!

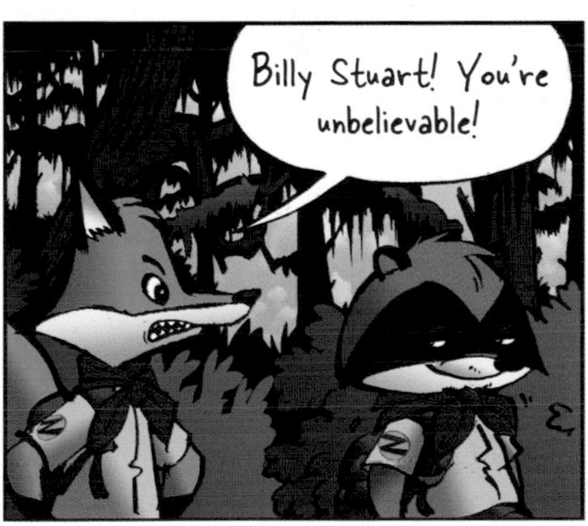
Billy Stuart! You're unbelievable!

I think about it. If I don't bring FrouFrou back to my neighbors, they won't want to pay me for my hard work.

And time keeps passing...Time! My grandfather Virgil. His time travels! I'm not out of the woods yet! I have an idea.

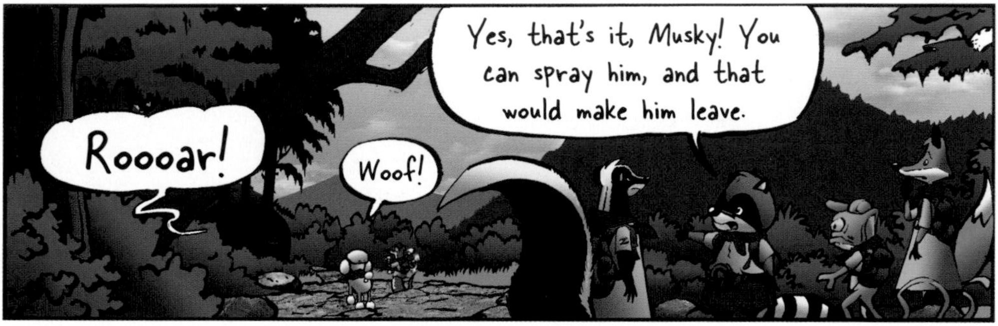
Rooooar!
Woof!
Yes, that's it, Musky! You can spray him, and that would make him leave.

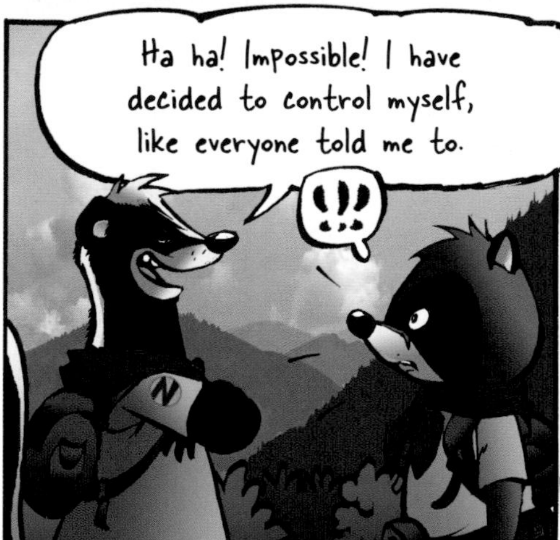
Ha ha! Impossible! I have decided to control myself, like everyone told me to.
!!!

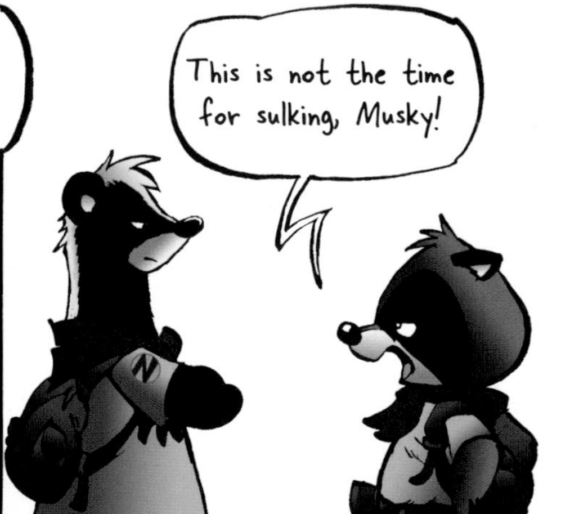
This is not the time for sulking, Musky!

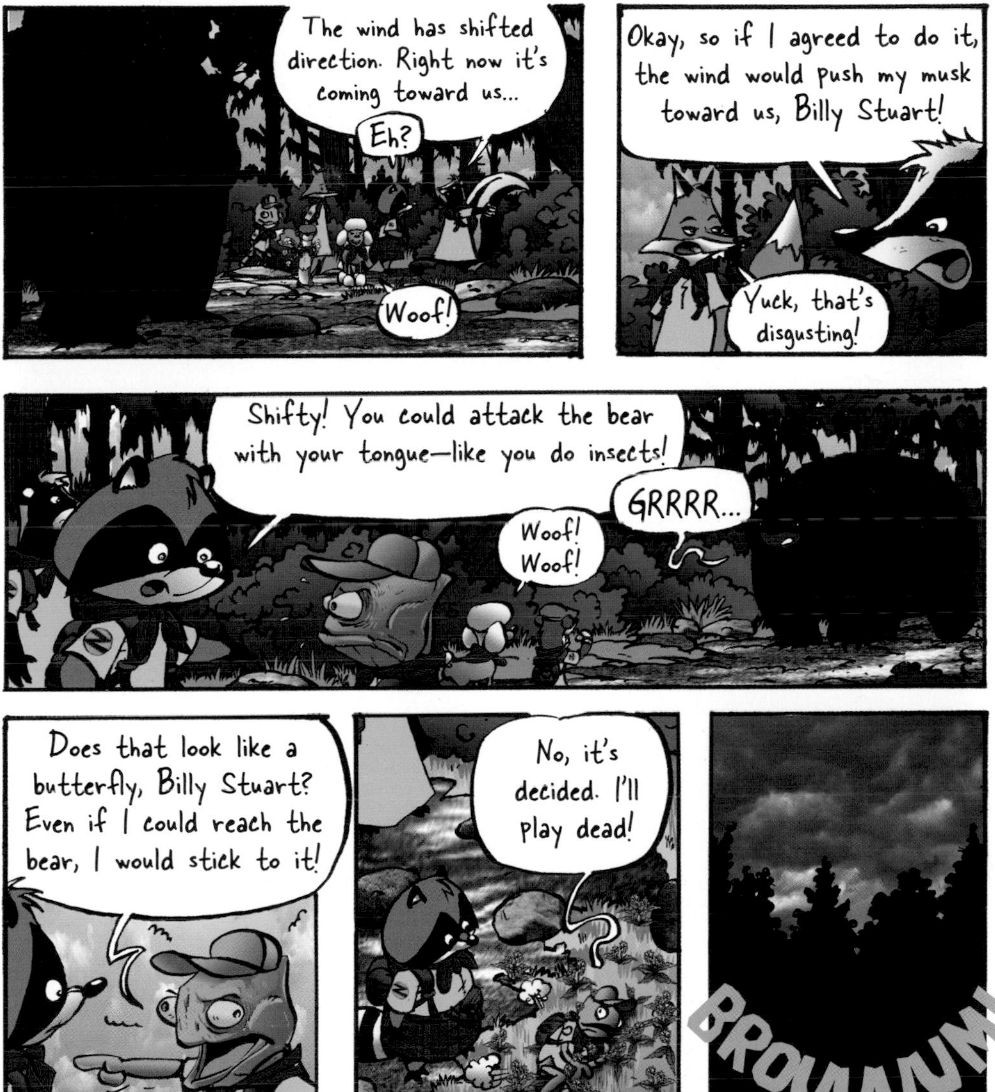
The wind has shifted direction. Right now it's coming toward us...
Eh?
Woof!
Okay, so if I agreed to do it, the wind would push my musk toward us, Billy Stuart!
Yuck, that's disgusting!
Shifty! You could attack the bear with your tongue—like you do insects!
Woof! Woof!
GRRRR...
Does that look like a butterfly, Billy Stuart? Even if I could reach the bear, I would stick to it!
No, it's decided. I'll play dead!
BROUUUUM!

He lies down on the ground, staying still like a stone ghoul.

Braooooooooom!

Another thunderclap, this one closer than the first. The sky is now in total darkness.

As if he has changed his mind, the bear retreats a few meters. He is visibly scared of the thunder.

BANG!

A violent noise explodes behind us, and we all jump. The bear turns on his heels and clears off back into the forest.

"Scaredy-cat!" Yeti yells defiantly.

"And that's what you call a job well done," announces Foxy, holding up two saucepans she has just clanged together.

Zzzzzz...zzzz...

That isn't thunder. It's Shifty snoring, lying on a bed of dandelions. The chameleon who has been playing dead has fallen asleep...so I wake him up.

"Shifty, with your white, your black and your yellow, you look like shepherd's pie," I tease.

For our friends, contrary to what you may have guessed, shepherd's pie is a traditional Scottish dish and has nothing to do with herding sheep. It is made with a layer of ground beef, a layer of mashed potato and a layer of cheese. It's delicious, according to some, and awful according to others.

"Ouaaaaaaah!" says the chameleon, stretching as he wakes up. "Did I miss anything?"

BRAAOOOOOOOOOUUUUUM!

The storm's rumblings are coming more and more frequently.

"Troop, let's hurry!" I say as the sky roars intensely right above us.

I estimate that we are at least five hundred meters from the spot where the river forks, the place my grandfather said he'd meet me.

"HALT!" Foxy thunders.

"Halt what?"

"Your dog, FrouFrou."

"It's not **MY** dog, Foxy! What language do I need to say it in?"

Foxy looks around.

The dog…

FrouFrou is gone!

TOPSY-TURVY

During their hike through Kanuks Forest, the Zintrepids encounter a **BEAR**. With a helping **HAND** from his friends, Billy gets through this challenge.

In the game Metagram (*meta*=transformation and *gram*=letter), you get from one word to another by changing one letter at a time, each time creating a new word. For example, you can get from WORD to CAVE like this: WORD—WORE—CORE—CARE—CAVE. Here's your challenge:

Turn the word BEAR into the word HAND. You will only need to create THREE words between BEAR and HAND.

Here are the points to remember:
You can only change one letter per word.

1. The letters have to stay in the same order.

2. Your words can be singular or plural.

3. Write down your words on a piece of paper. You will be able to see the solution more clearly.

Solution on page 158.

In Belcher's Cavern

Now, where was I?

Ah yes! The BLACK BEAR has vanished back into the wild. The storm is about to worsen, and there is no shelter in sight. And my grandfather is due to start his time-travel trip soon.

That's where I was!

Oh yeah, I almost forgot—it's also started to rain.

But what am I worried about? Am I really worried about a stupid white poodle who has disappeared in a FOREST?

I round up the Zintrepids.

"Troop, let's prioritize. First, let's find shelter. We'll deal with the dog later."

"There are some CAVES a bit farther along the river. We could take cover there," suggests Foxy.

"Okay!"

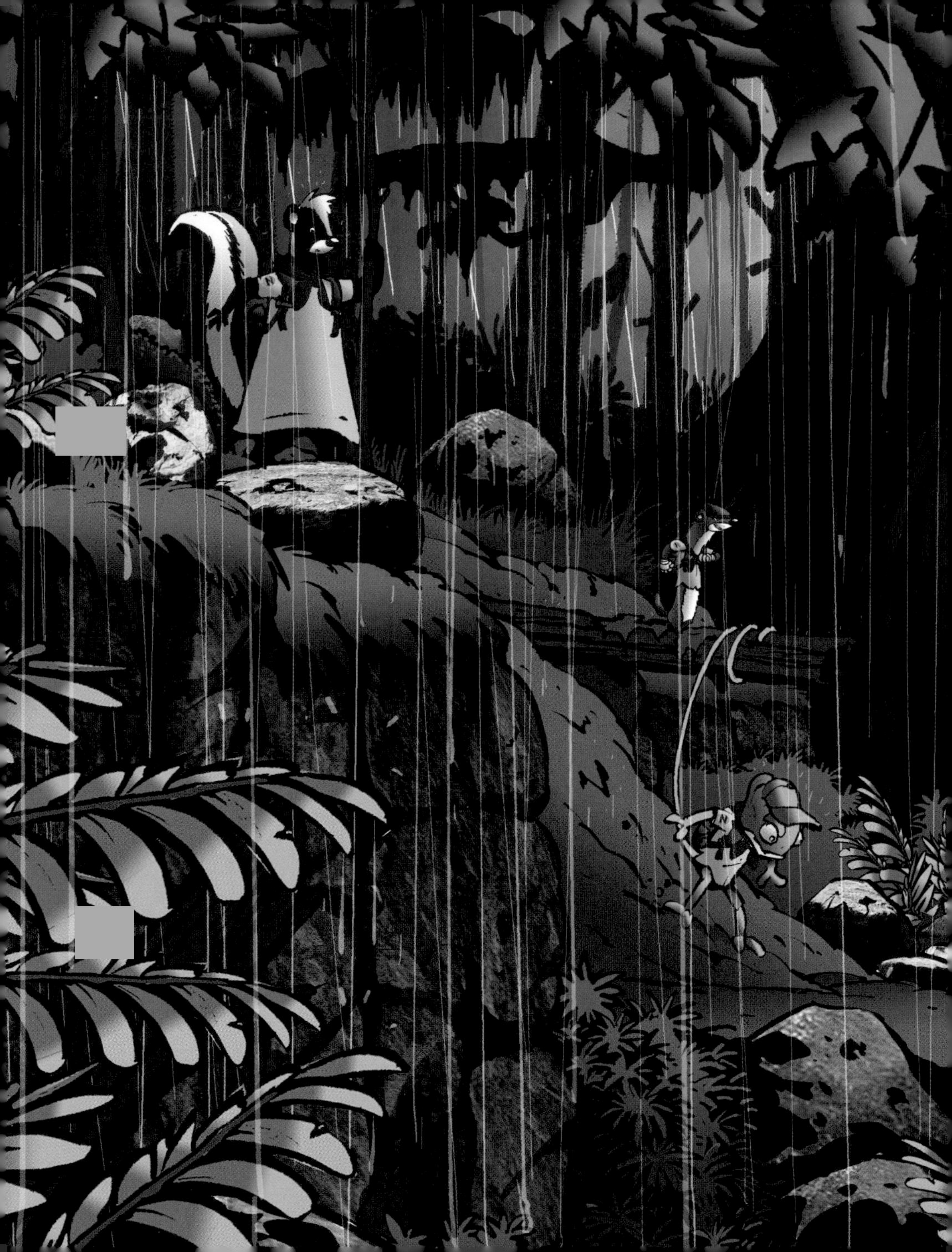

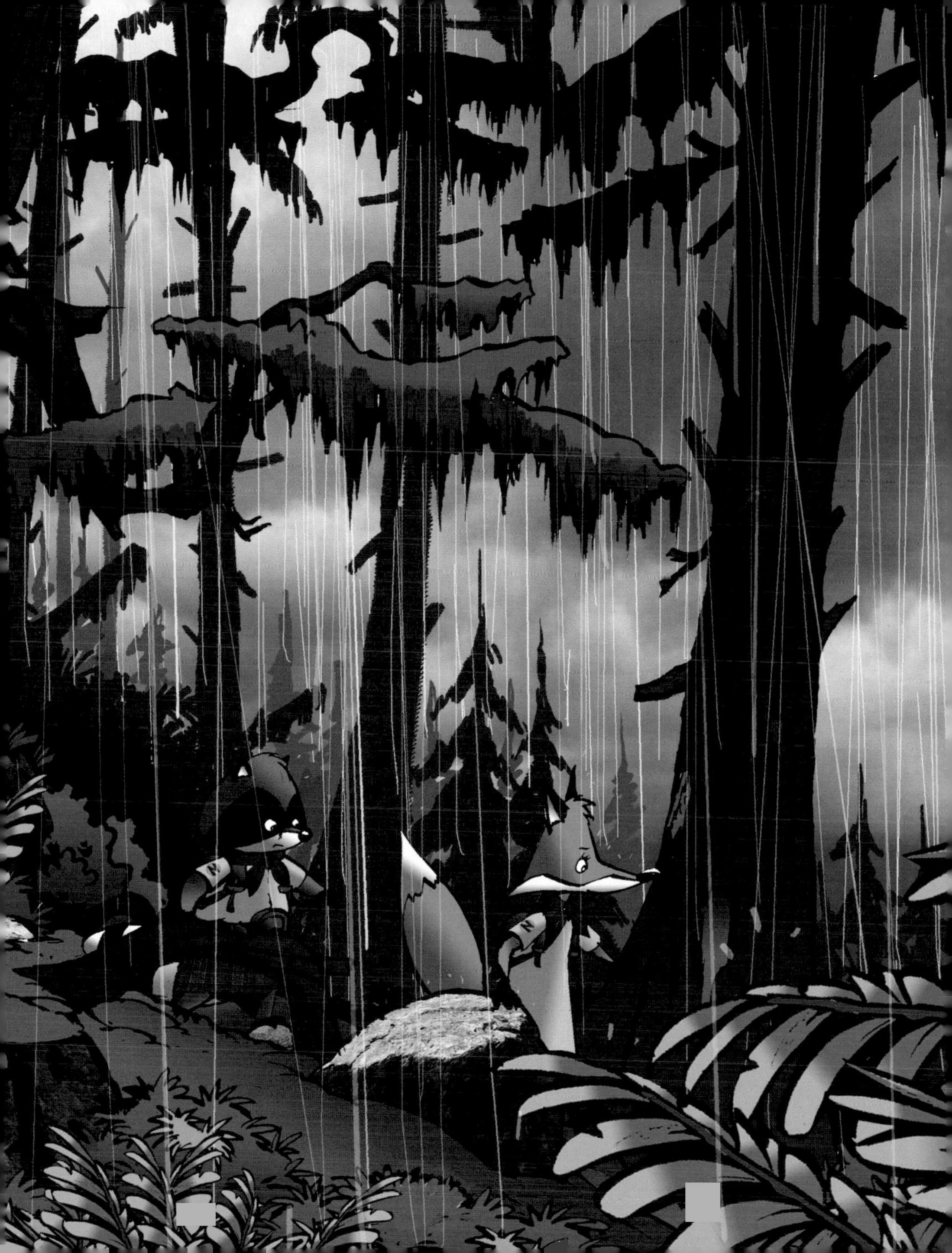

We are in the area of Belcher's Cavern. My grandfather might already be here somewhere. I hope so.

THE STORM WORSENS. The trail is wet and slippery. With every step we are in danger of falling. The thunder rolls on relentlessly in the furious sky. Suddenly Foxy stops, causing a pileup.

"**Listen!**" orders the fox, cupping her ear.

"What? I can only hear the thunder!" we say.

"**Be quiet!**" she orders.

Despite the storm's racket, we could just about make out some faint barks.

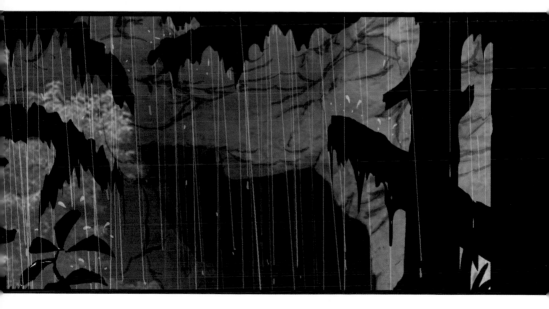

"FrouFrou! Straight ahead!" yells Foxy.

I'm offended.

"Hey, I'm the leader of the pack."

"You're right. Excuse me, Billy Stuart," the fox says with an exasperated sigh.

Satisfied at having re-established our hierarchy, I move forward.

"TROOP!"

The trail descends and branches to the left. The dog's barks get closer. The swollen river is almost overflowing its banks.

It's raining so hard that it's difficult to see where we are going. It feels like we're in the shower!

I can make out an **ENORMOUS** dark mass. Oh no! The black bear is back! And he looks even bigger! Unless he went back to get his mother…

I wait for the roar of an attack.

Woof! Woof! Woof!

Black bears don't go *woof*! Dogs do! It's—

"FrouFrou!" cries Foxy, happy to be reunited with her love.

I realize my mistake. The dark mass is, in fact, the entry to the cave. FrouFrou has been taking shelter there and barked to lead us to him.

At last we are dry!

Foxy rewards FrouFrou with a cuddle. The poodle dances up and down on his hind legs, proudly barking with **pleasure**. He comes to me, hoping to get the same reward.

What if the black bear followed the dog—or worse, what if this cave is his home? FrouFrou would have led us right into the lion's den! Um, the bear's den?

We are in danger.

"Hey, look what I found!" yells Shifty.

The chameleon holds up a leather notebook with golden letters on the cover. They read:

XS

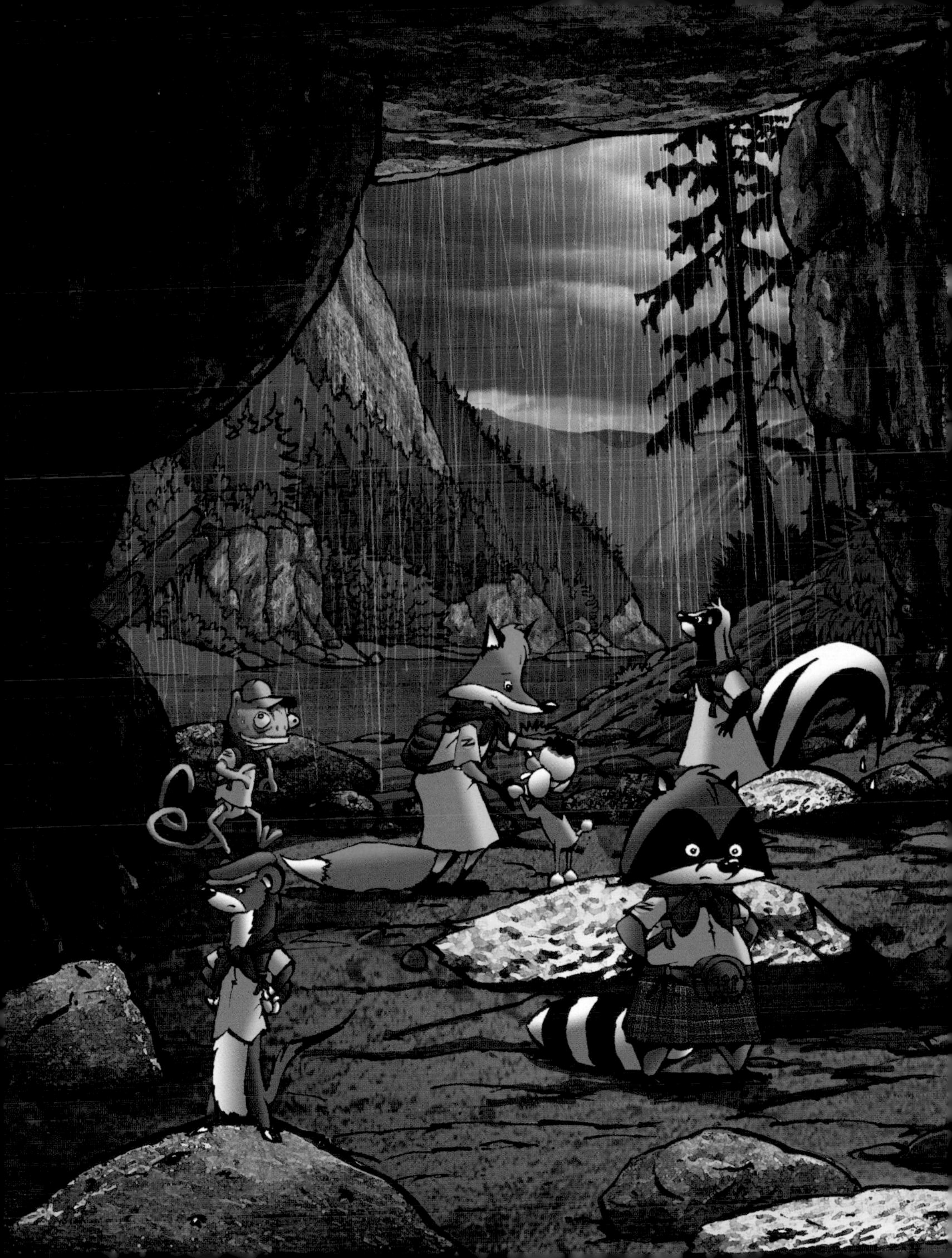

I think about it. The cave…the meeting…*XS*…

I look at the cover again.

"It's not **XS**—it's **YS**! Like Virgil Stuart!"

"Your grandfather!" exclaims Musky.

Overwhelmed, I open the notebook.

"Read it later, Billy Stuart," says Foxy. "We have a **serious problem**."

What could be more important than my grandfather Virgil's notebook?

Our lives!

The river is overflowing and filling up the cave, **slowly** but surely!

Operation Get Us Out of Here!

There is no way out! The river has become a torrent that has already reached the mouth of the cave. Soon our shelter will be flooded.

I make my hands into a **mega**phon**e** to be heard over the noise of the storm and the river.

"Troop, we have to find a new exit."

"Let's try this," says Foxy.

She points toward A DARK PASSAGEWAY that climbs toward the back of the cave.

Musky has brought her flashlight. Me too. We plunge deeper into the cave. After a short climb we hike downward. The low ceiling forces us to stoop.

Again I entrust the dog to Foxy, because they love each other so much! She keeps the poodle on his leash.

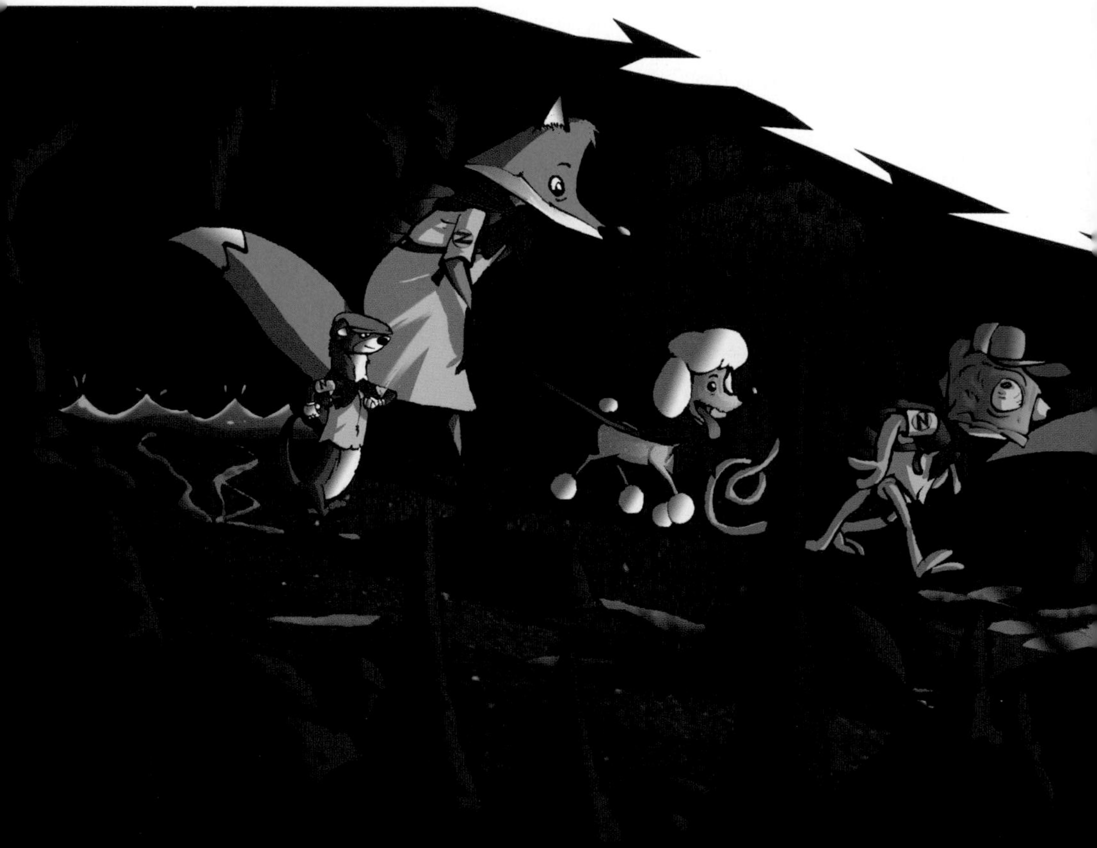

Awful thoughts plague me. I try to chase them away, but they keep coming back. Who says there will *be* an opening at the other end? It could be a dead end! And what if water keeps filling the cave? We will be trapped! This is awful!

I'm finding it difficult to breathe. Is this anxiety? Am I claustrophobic?

Claustrophobia is the fear of enclosed spaces. Warning: Fridges and clothes dryers are enclosed spaces and should be completely avoided.

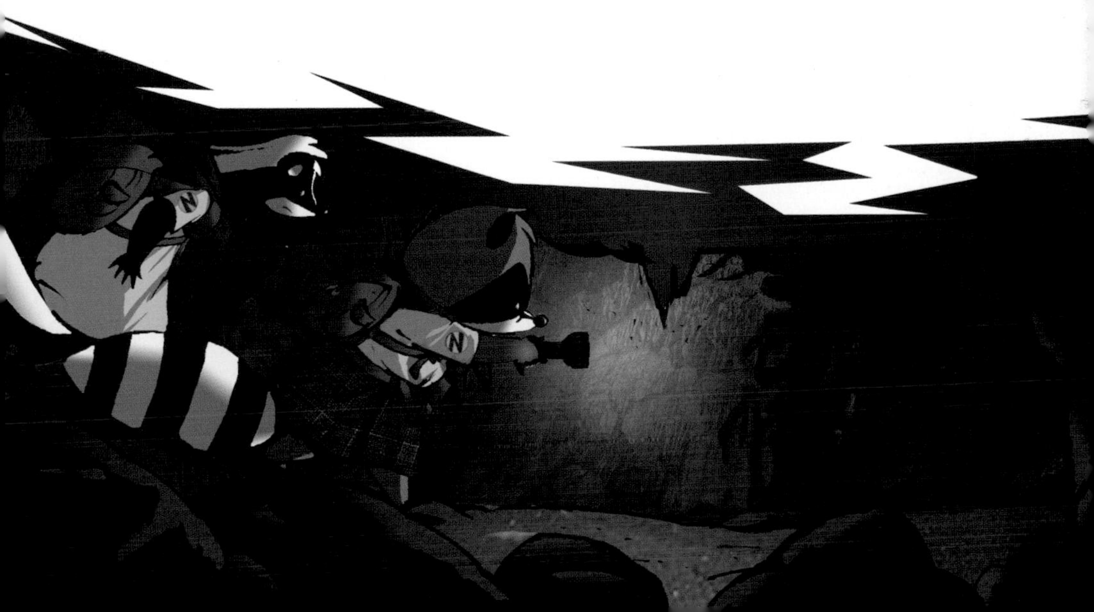

The dog is barking in fits and starts. **Silly animal!**

He thinks he is replying to another dog, but it is his own bark echoing off the walls of the cave.

The Barking Concerto is never-ending.

"Make him be quiet, Foxy!" I beg.

"Your dog is nervous."

After a few minutes of walking, the trail **goes up** and the path widens. The suffocating sensation that has been bothering me wanes. We can finally walk upright. When I raise my arms, I no longer touch the roof. When I stretch them sideways, I don't touch the walls of the passageway. I can breathe easier. Whew! I'm not anxious anymore.

"FrouFrou!" cries Foxy.

She dropped the leash for only a second, but the dog seized his chance to escape.

I am starting to feel anxious again! The dog is now at the crossroads of two paths. He is panting and seems nervous— very unlike him!

Which path to choose?

The notebook! I take it out of my bag and look through it, using the beam from **my flashlight**. My grandfather explored this cavern, mapping it as he went along.

Hmm. Virgil Stuart was a **great** explorer but a terrible illustrator. On the third page of the notebook is a crudely drawn map of the river and the entrance to Belcher's Cavern.

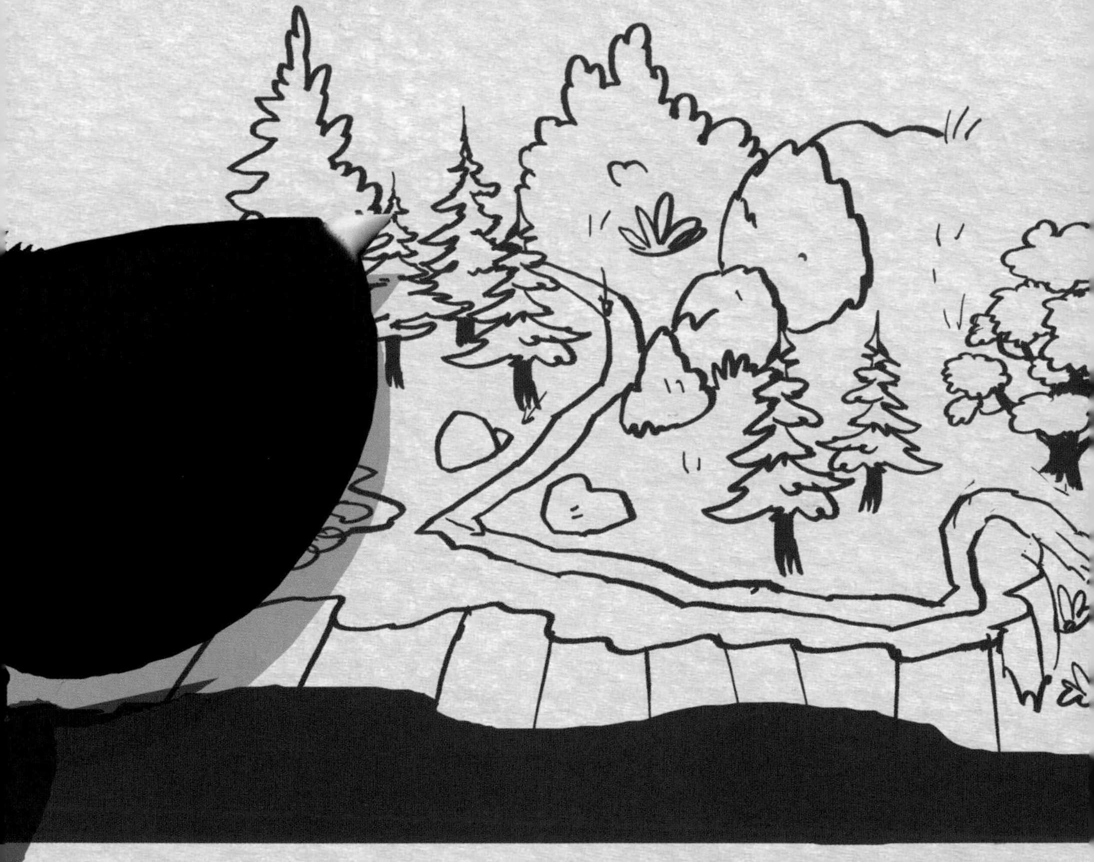

The Zintrepids are unaware of how the cave got its name. It's named after the explorer George M. Belcher, who discovered the spot more than a hundred years ago. The legend is that Belcher disappeared mysteriously while exploring the cavern. According to this legend, which has been forgotten now but was mentioned in journals of the time, a mysterious creature haunts the area. Little kids think the name Belcher refers to belching—they find it hilarious to hear their burps echoing through its chambers.

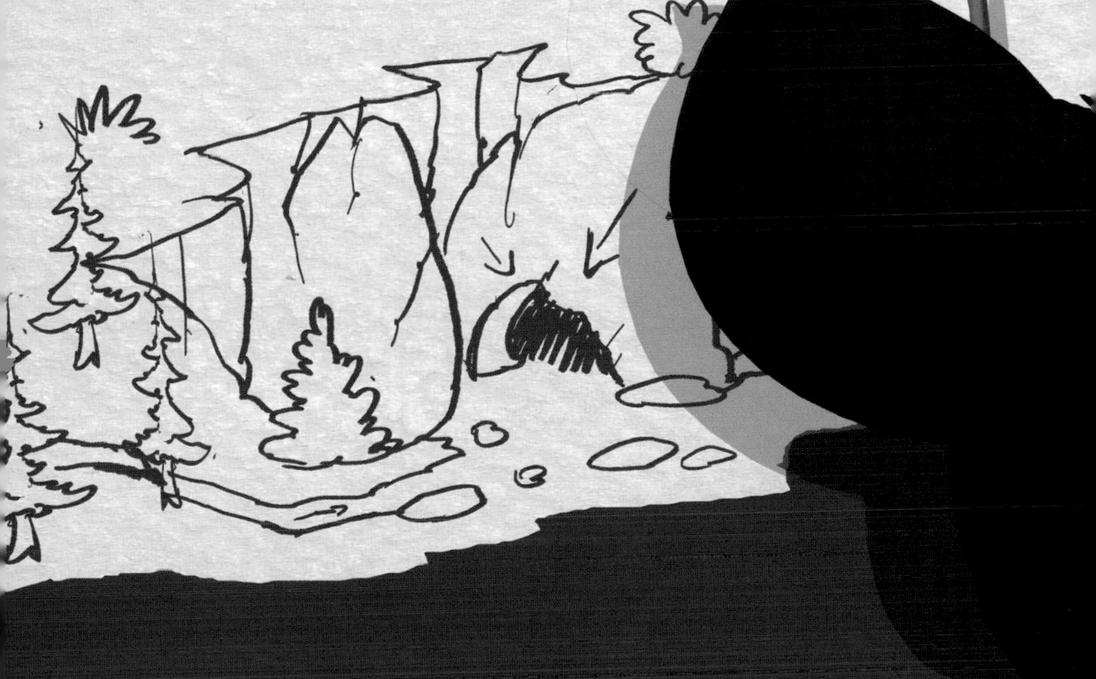

So we're here, where the tunnel forks...
I'd opt for the tunnel to the left.
That X could be telling us where not to go.
Or that's where the treasure is buried!
It's well known! On all treasure maps, the X marks the spot where the treasure is hidden. Didn't you guys read The Little Pirates?

It's not like there is an arrow in the right tunnel.
Kabillions of crusty-clawed crawfish in that Bulstrode River!
What do you think, Billy Stuart?

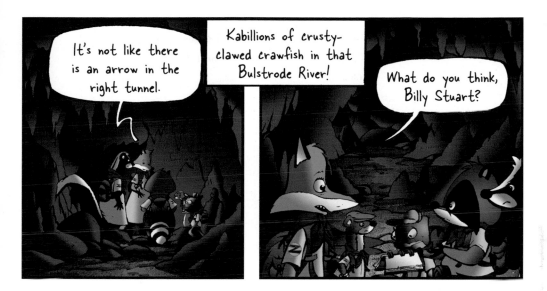

I shrug my shoulders, pretending I don't know.

But in fact I have just figured it out. This famous X doesn't represent a treasure. It marks the beginning of my grandfather's journey. It isn't an X but a V, done in a hurry. A V with a tiny, involuntary extension at the bottom that has caused confusion.

V as in voyage.

V as in voyaging in time.

V as in Virgil…

WHO AM I?

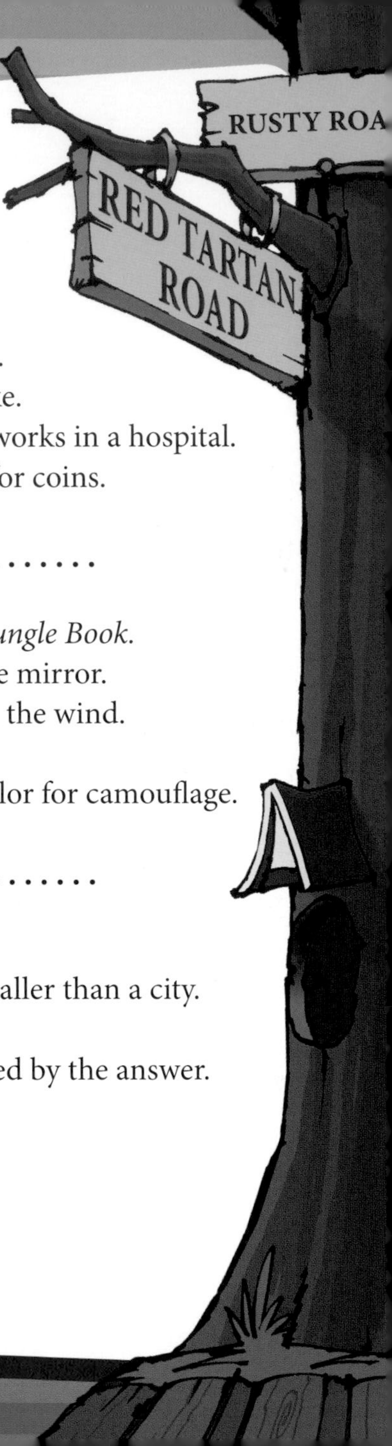
RUSTY ROA
RED TARTAN ROAD

My beginning is the sound of a happy cat.
My ending is the sound of a grumpy snake.
I rhyme with the name of someone who works in a hospital.
Put me together and I am a handy place for coins.

My first is the name of the snake in *The Jungle Book.*
My second is who I see when I look in the mirror.
My third is the side that is sheltered from the wind.
My last is the opposite of "off."
Put me together and watch me change color for camouflage.

My first is another word for donkey.
My second is bigger than a village but smaller than a city.
My third is no longer alive.
Put me together and you might be shocked by the answer.

Solution on page 158.

Chapter 9

On the Right Track?

Should I tell the Zintrepids what I have figured out? Let's wait to see what happens first…

I missed a detail when I first looked at my grandfather's map. If I am judging correctly the path of the river that goes around the cavern in the drawing, then the tunnel to the **RIGHT** goes toward an exit. When the storm calms down and the river returns to its banks, we will be able to use this tunnel. And eventually we could find ourselves back out in the forest.

On the other hand, if we **LEFT**, who knows where we could end up?

It's only right for me to let my friends know.

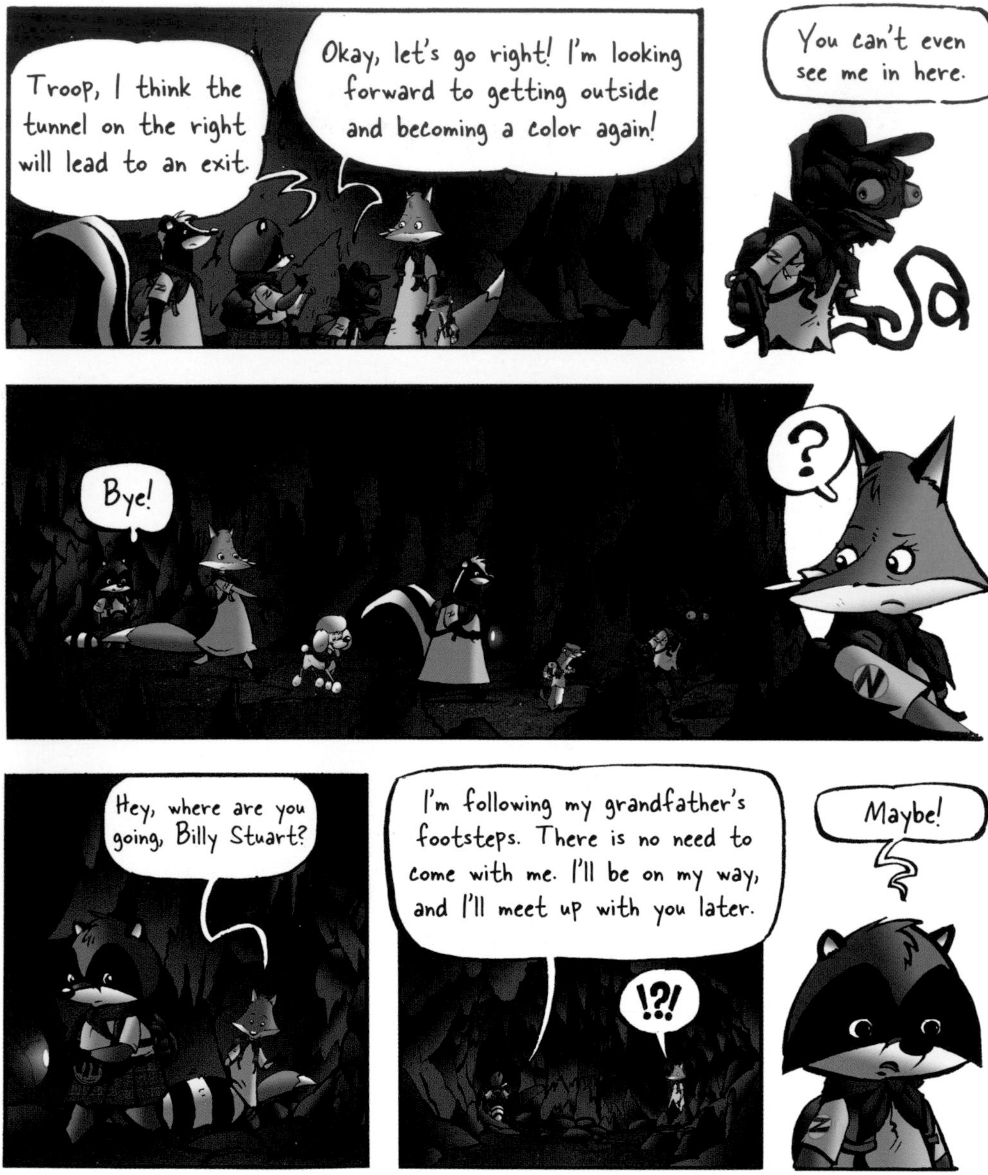

Troop, I think the tunnel on the right will lead to an exit.
Okay, let's go right! I'm looking forward to getting outside and becoming a color again!
You can't even see me in here.
Bye!
?
Hey, where are you going, Billy Stuart?
I'm following my grandfather's footsteps. There is no need to come with me. I'll be on my way, and I'll meet up with you later.
!?!
Maybe!

With my flashlight, I go deeper into the tunnel. Immediately I feel very alone.

I resist the urge to turn around.

To give myself courage, I sing the Zintrepids' anthem:

"We are marching toward adventure
Proud and strong..."

Useless. The echo of my voice is scaring me more than soothing me.

In my mind, I see my grandfather's map. Was it drawn to scale? I don't know. I do know, however, that on paper the tunnel on the left, the one with the Y, is shorter than the one on the right.

In theory, I should soon arrive at the spot marked by the famous Y. What will happen then? Will my body be shaken by violent vibrations? Will I be **transported** in time? Will I lose consciousness? Will I be struck with a **blinding clarity**? Will I—

KABILLIONS of crusty-clawed crawfish in that Bulstrode River!

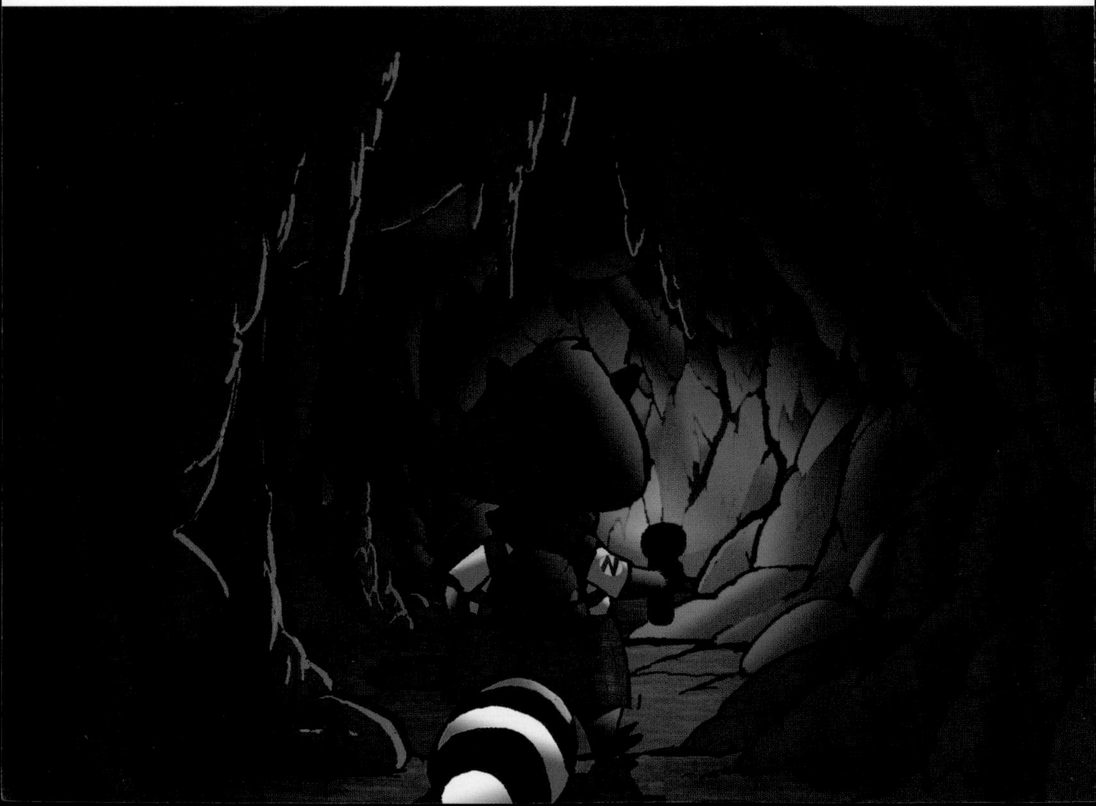

Reality catches up with me. This is awful!

I am alone, underground, pacing a dark tunnel that in all likelihood is populated by insects hoping for one thing—that my flashlight batteries will die so they can attack me and eat me alive.

I shiver from head to toe. On the edge of panic, I stop walking.

Time travel is impossible! In believing my grandfather's nonsense, I am now in danger of losing *myself* in this cavern. I should have listened to my mother!

Besides, is this even Belcher's Cavern? There are many caves along the river. The notebook *was* found here, but a wild animal might have found it and brought it here.

My heart beats faster. It was a mistake to separate from the troop. Not just a mistake. It was full-blown **craziness!!**

I even miss FrouFrou. I—

What? Me miss FrouFrou?

That's it. I have lost my mind! No doubt I have a case of the "dark-cave crazies."

I have to get going. If I hurry, I can rejoin the group. Yes. I will backtrack.

"Ouch!"

I've hit something.

I shine my flashlight.

The tunnel…

There isn't one anymore.

I've bumped smack into a wall!

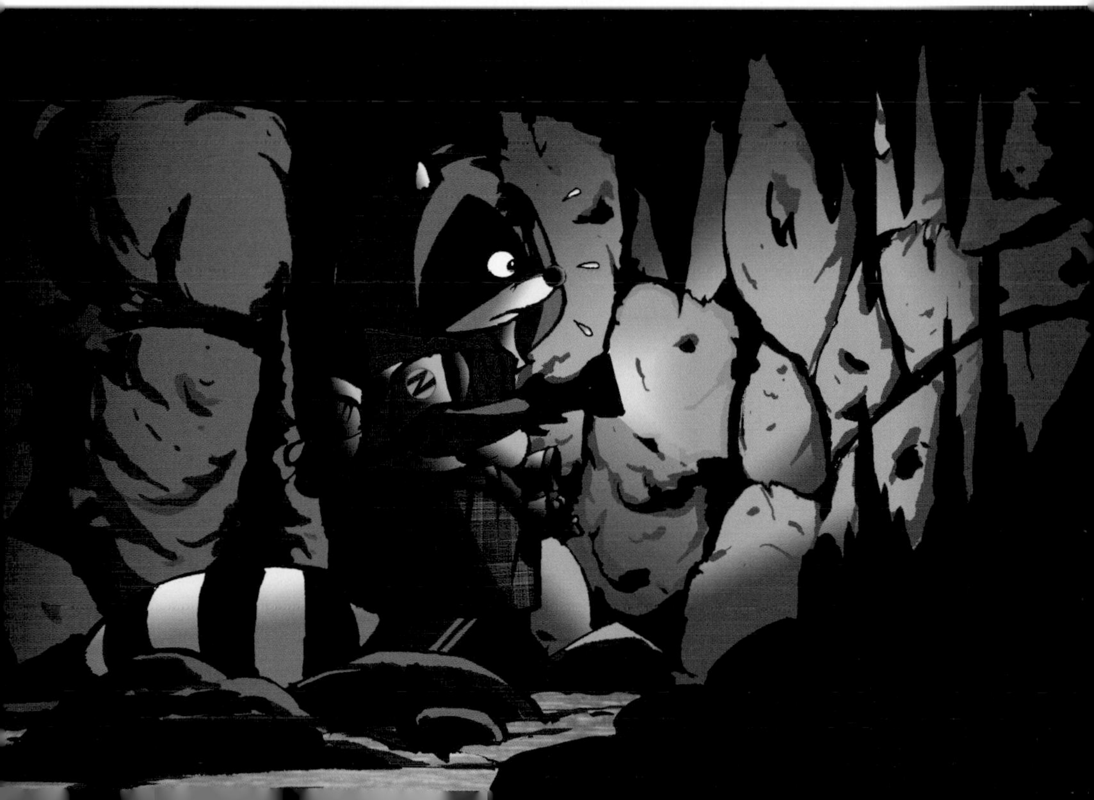

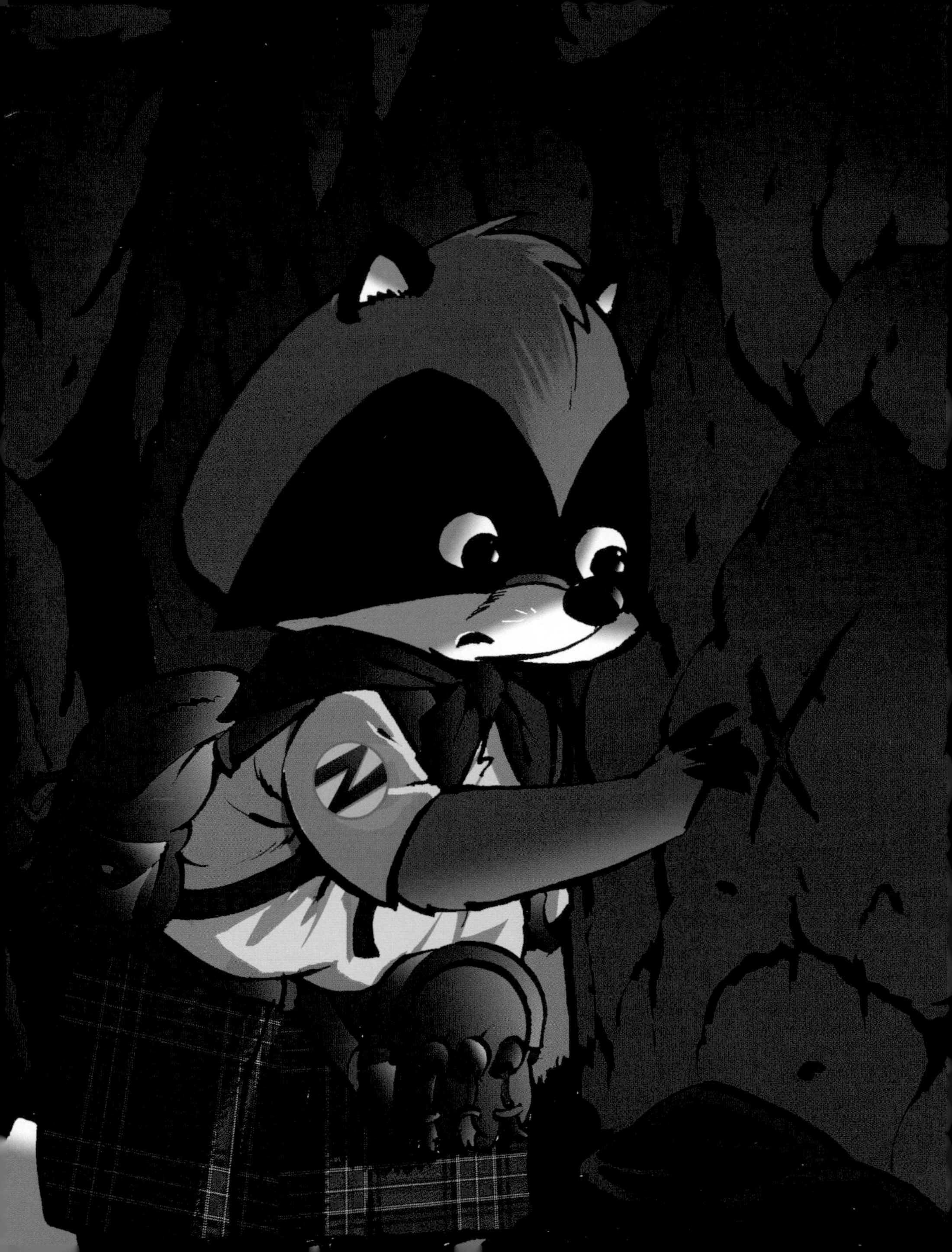

On the Other Side of the Wall

I am trapped! I can feel the wall in front of me—there are no exits. I bang on it a few times, hurting my hand, and I **yell**, even though I don't believe anyone will hear me.

"Is there someone on the other side? Troop! Come help me! I'm here!"

Here? I'm trying not to think about where *here* is.

My efforts are pointless. I have the **UNCOMFORTABLE** feeling of being separated from my friends by more than just a rock wall.

Feeling along the wall, my fingers graze something **engraved in the stone**. I don't need to shine my flashlight on it to know what it is. My fingers read the Y that, written in a hurry, so many could confuse with an X.

Y as in voyage and Virgil.

My grandfather has left his mark. And then? What *if*…
I mean, why not?

Open sesame!

In my head, I picture the wall rising slowly, and I am able
go back home. Nothing rises. I guess I'm not a descendant of
Ali Baba and his forty raccoons. I have made a mistake and can
no longer go back. I continue my **exploration** of the cave.

My worries have a mind of their own. What **if** I hit another dead end? I would be at an impasse. Or what **if** I go the wrong way and I end up stuck underground? Isn't that what I've already done?

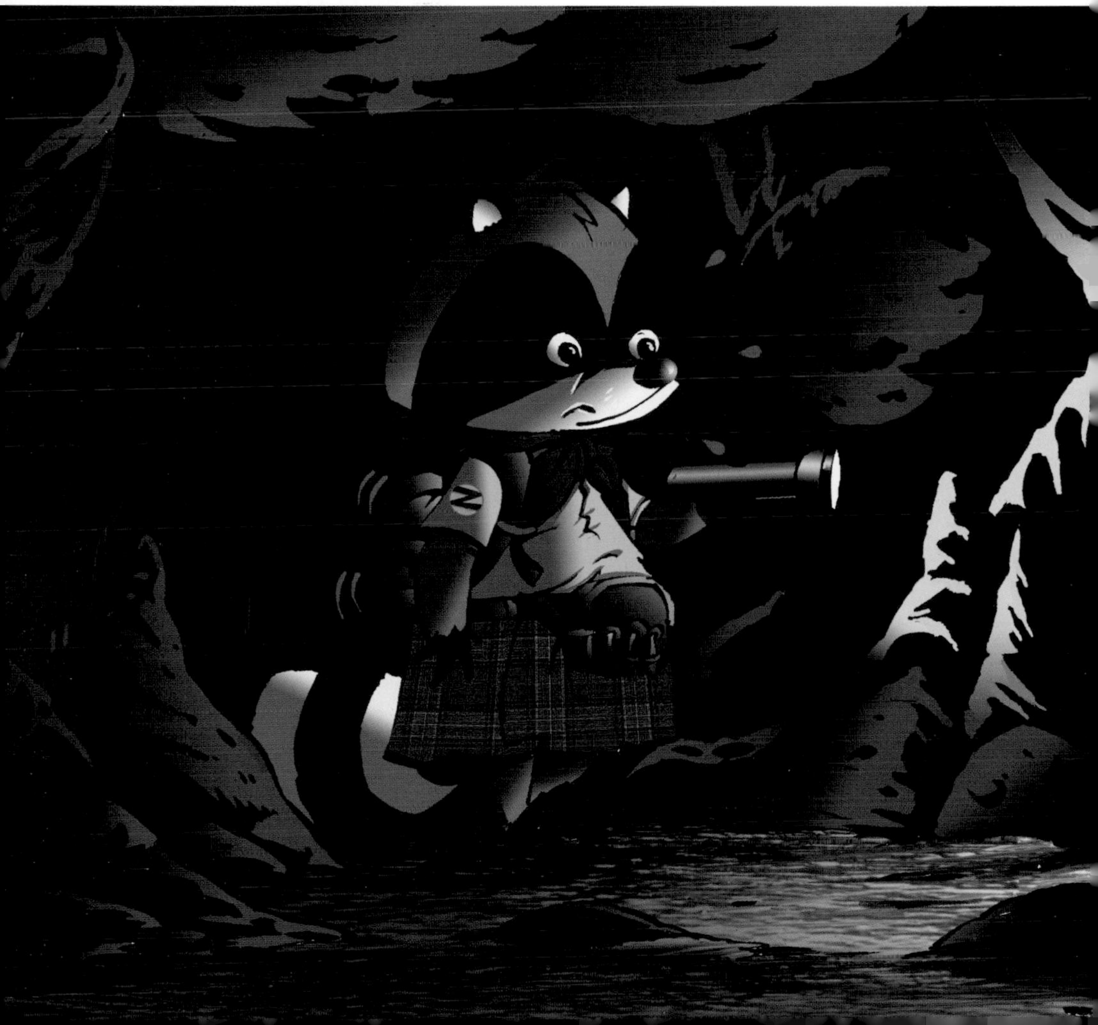

I am having difficulty breathing. Suddenly, in my frenzied state, I have a comforting thought. My grandfather Virgil left proof that he came this way. His inscription in the stone is the proof—living proof. Yes, he must be alive, my grandfather. I just have to find him.

This thought gives me the strength to continue.

Right up until the moment my flashlight batteries die, leaving me in the **PITCH BLACK**. I cry out in despair.

"**HELLLLLLLLLPPPPPPPPPPPPPP!**"

HELLP...HELLLP...HELLLPPPPPP, mimics my echo.

I must stay calm—though if it weren't for my Stuart pride, I would burst into tears! No! I'm mad now! All of this is the fault of…FrouFrou! Taking care of the dog these past few days has taken so much energy that I forgot to recharge my flashlight batteries.

Oh yeah! Batteries! I have the gadget to recharge them in my bag! **HURRAH!** I shouldn't be so hard on the poodle. Now, I only have to find a plug…in this cave…to rechar—

Idiot!

Yes, it is still all the fault of that dirty pooch!

guilty
his fault
dirty pooch
responsible

I gather what is left of my courage to face the **DARKNESS** and, groping along the wall, move forward. My eyes slowly get used to the dark. Following the winding path I come to a bend where, finally, I feel a glimmer of hope. The tunnel is bathed in semidarkness—I can see the walls.

I pick up my pace, wanting to get out as soon as possible. It feels like it's been **centuries** since the Zintrepids took refuge in the cave. But is this still the same cave?

Yes!

Uh…no! I don't actually know the answer to that question. I mean yes as in, **HURRAH! SUPER! EUREKA!** *Yessssss!* Because there is light at the end of the tunnel. My worries ease.

I start running toward freedom.

BING!

Suddenly I am hit with a violent *knock* to my head. I see stars.

I am lying on the ground, stunned. What an uncomfortable position! I am sore on my front. I am sore on my back. And my fingers feel a big bump on my skull.

Ouch! Ouch! Ouch!

Painfully I stand up. I can barely keep my balance. With eyes half shut, I look around for my assailant. There is no one else in the tunnel. I realize the cause of my **anguish**— a stalactite hanging from the tunnel's ceiling. I should have been more careful and not gone barreling forward into the unknown, especially with this low ceiling.

A good lesson for the future.

At least I didn't crash into a stalagmite, I tell myself!

You know the difference, right? Stalactites come down from the ceiling, and stalagmites grow from the ground. Simple and true.

I move around the offending stalactite and keep walking, stooping just in case.

After just a few minutes I come out of the tunnel. **KABILLIONS** of crusty-clawed crawfish in that Bulstrode River!

The tunnel has led me into an immense underground opening! A chamber!

I have no idea how long I stand there, staring into the chamber. I might still be there if I hadn't heard a **quivering** voice behind me.

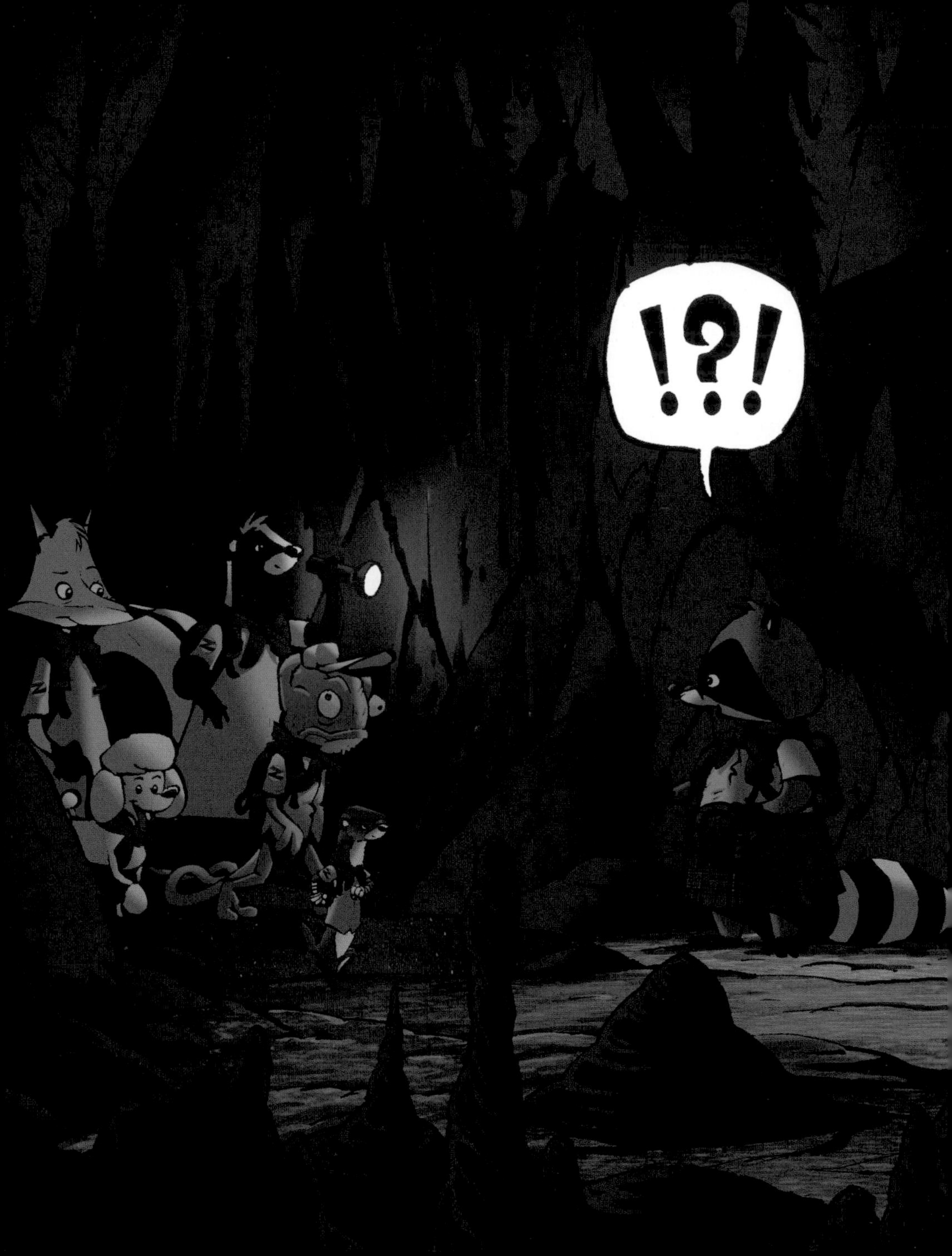
!?!

Chapter 11

Unexpected Reunions

If I'd seen Santa Claus in a kilt, I wouldn't have been more surprised.

"Troop, what are you doing here?"

I pinch myself just to be sure I'm not seeing things. My friends have found me! FrouFrou dances on his hind legs, excited to see me after our brief separation.

"Calm down, dog!" I tell him in my most authoritative voice—to no avail, of course.

The poodle sniffs everywhere without straying too far. It's not that I'm disappointed to be reunited with the Zintrepids. I am shocked. Yes. Shocked!

"We're happy to find you too," says Foxy sarcastically.

Musky points to a spot right under our noses.

"Where are we? Is this still Belcher's Cavern?" she asks.

I don't have the answer. But I need to know how they ended up here, with me.

"When we were at the crossroads of the two tunnels, I took the ◁ **LEFT** passage to follow my grandfather's path. You, you took the path to the **RIGHT** ▷ to find the exit."

Foxy tells me what happened. "Your dog—"

I sigh. Why am I not surprised?

"He's not **My** dog—"

"Stop interrupting me, Billy Stuart! We went to the right, but after a few minutes FrouFrou figured out you were missing. What could we do?"

"You two are inseparable! He escaped and started tracking you. We all followed him!"

"Yeah," grumbles Musky. "You know, I almost bumped into a stalagmite. I spotted it at the last second. Shifty, he didn't see it."

The chameleon rolls his eyes. "Ouch! Ouch! Ouch!"

"And here we are with you. The troop is reunited," says Foxy. But that doesn't mean we know where we are.

"Why don't you look at your notebook?" suggests Yeti. "It must have something about the spot where we are right now."

That's true. I hadn't thought of that. I turn to the page where the cavern map is drawn.

YES! My grandfather has written something: *Get yourself to the heart of the city's maze. You will find there the clue for the next part of your journey.*

"That means nothing! **MY EYES CAN'T BELIEVE THEIR EARS**," yells Shifty.

"Is there anything else?" asks Foxy. "Is there something about Belcher's Cavern?"

I leaf through the notebook. No. Only **blank** pages.

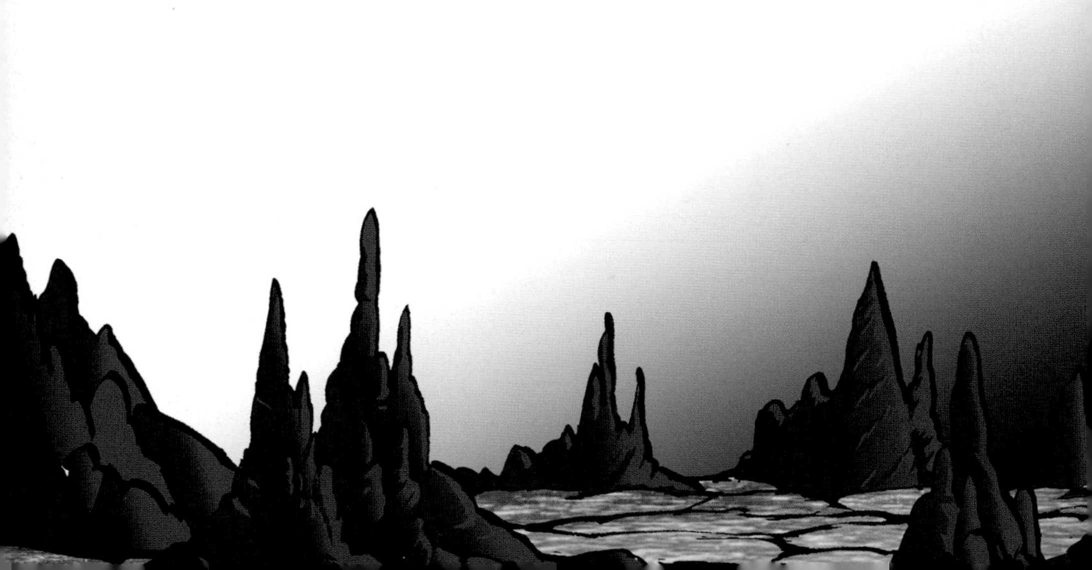

Chapter 12

"Scriiiii!"

Surrounded by my friends and dog, I look around the chamber. What can I possibly compare it to? I've never seen anything like it. It is **way** bigger than our school's gymnasium in every way—height, width **and** depth.

If we were playing **basketball**, running from one end to another, you'd die of fatigue or hunger before getting to the other team's basket. I'm not exaggerating.

If you were to install a light on the ceiling, you'd have to get on a helicopter to change the burned-out bulb. I'm not exaggerating at all.

There are some amusing coincidences in life. At the very moment I am writing this paragraph, a helicopter is flying over my house on Gray Road! Seriously! You can't make this stuff up.

But a ceiling light in here would be useless—it would never be bright enough for this space. The chamber is bathed in darkness. But for reasons I am ignoring, probably luminous mushrooms, we can see well enough to distinguish details like the inescapable STALACTITES and STALAGMITES.

I can't help but exclaim, "KABILLIONS of crusty-clawed crawfish in that Bulstrode River!"

. . .iver. . . .ver. . . ver. . .

My voice reverberates to all corners of the ginormous chamber. I think if there had been someone way off at the other end, and I had even just murmured, they would have been able to hear me. The sound in here carries easily.

To conserve the batteries in her flashlight, Musky turns it off.

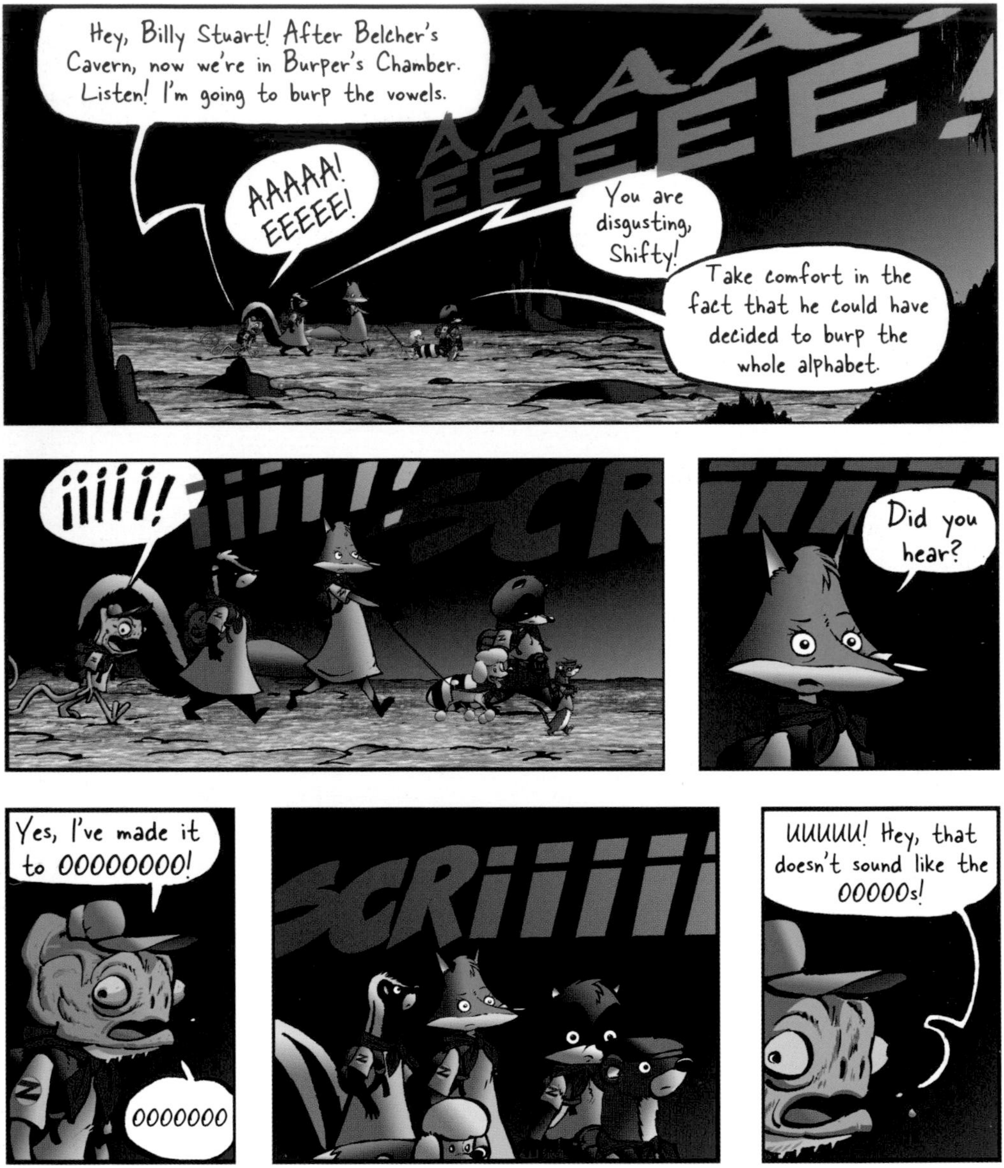
Hey, Billy Stuart! After Belcher's Cavern, now we're in Burper's Chamber. Listen! I'm going to burp the vowels.
AAAAA! EEEEE!
You are disgusting, Shifty!
Take comfort in the fact that he could have decided to burp the whole alphabet.
iiiii!
Did you hear?
Yes, I've made it to OOOOOOOO!
OOOOOOO
SCRiiiii
UUUUU! Hey, that doesn't sound like the OOOOOs!

We move forward cautiously and quietly, trying to figure out where the strange cry came from. I suddenly realize that wc have been spotted by something. The ground around us is littered with stalagmites, so there are a few spots we could hide if we needed to.

"Eyes! Over there!" says Foxy, pointing to a corner of the chamber.

"Are you sure?" whispers Musky.

"Yes! There is a pair of them."

"Good news! At least we know it's not a Cyclops we're dealing with," says Shifty.

And the eyes are very **RED**...

All of a sudden FrouFrou gets on his hind legs and starts barking furiously. Foxy tightens her hold on the poodle's leash. Above our heads we hear a rapid beating of wings. A **SHADOW** passes. There is something up there!

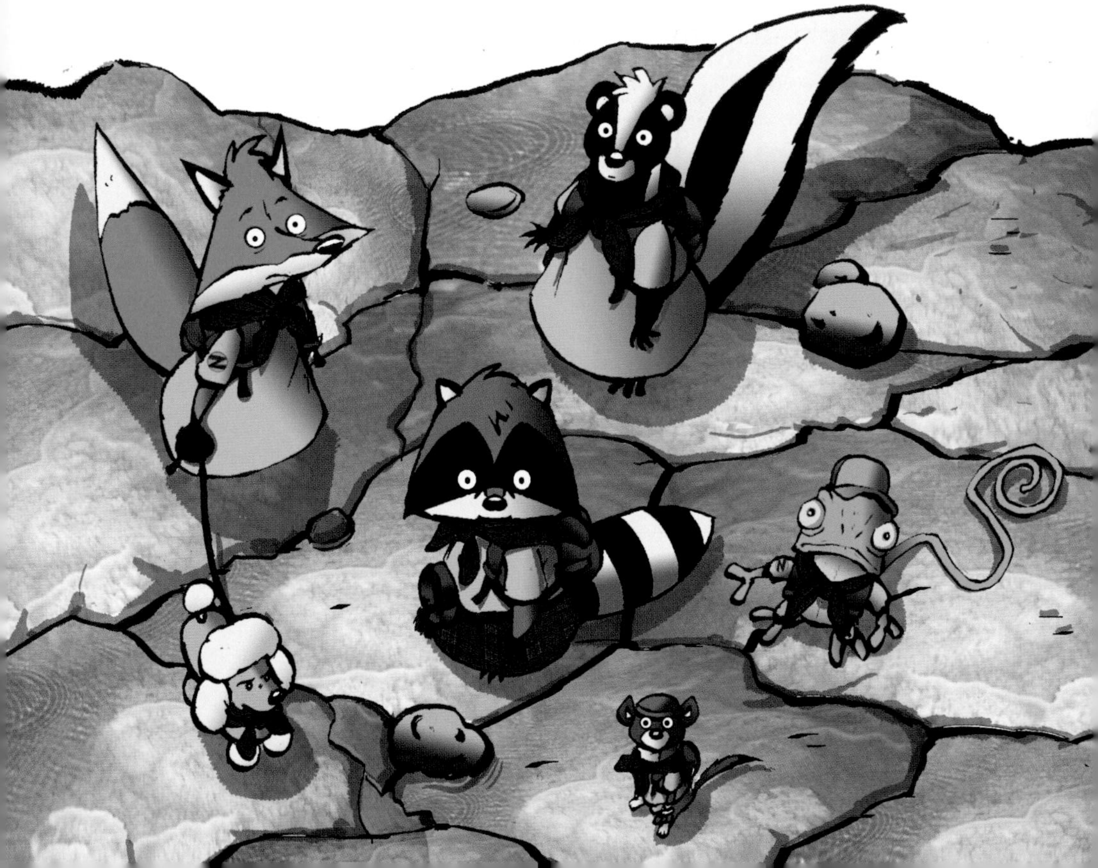

Chapter 13

Batman

"What if, instead of Belcher's Cavern, we are in 's Cavern?" Shifty suggests.

"You read too many comics," Musky says.

Bring it on! No, really—bring it on!

"Yuck! I stepped on something," complains Musky, shaking her foot.

She lifts her paw. It is **DRIPPING** with a whitish goo, half liquid, half solid, and it does not smell like **roses**.

"Guano," states Foxy, keeping her distance.

"That confirms the presence of Batman," Shifty joins in. "It's Batman guano."

Guano is the name given to the excrement of marine birds and bats. Note: Batman does not produce guano in his secret quarters. He does it in the toilet.

"Clearly, we are in a cavern populated by bats," Foxy says.

"Ughh!" cries Musky, pulling her head into her shoulders. "I don't want them getting caught in my fur."

Of course, that's only a myth. Bats don't try to get caught in people's hair or in skunks' fur. Neither does Batman.

"Don't be frightened," says Shifty reassuringly. "After all, it might be that we are dealing with vampire bats, in which case it's not your head they will go for, but your neck!"

"I should have worn a wool scarf and a garlic-bulb neck-lace," the skunk says with regret.

"Troop! Let's hurry and get out of here."

We quicken our pace, checking over our shoulders the whole time as we move through the cavern.

"Does someone know where we are going?" asks Yeti. He is riding the dog, who seems happy to be carrying him.

"You could walk!" scolds Foxy. "He's a poodle, not a PONY."

"He wants to carry me," the weasel replies. "Isn't that true, FrouFrou?"

He pats the dog's flank. FrouFrou responds by wagging his tail.

I am the leader of the Zintrepids. And my intuition tells me we should go straight ahead, that there will surely be an exit at the end of this cavern. Something tells me this is the way my grandfather Virgil came.

STOP!

Surprised, FrouFrou jumps, throwing Yeti off. The weasel just manages to avoid falling over a cliff, thanks to Musky's quick reflexes—she grabs Yeti by his bandana.

Directly in front of us is a giant crevasse.

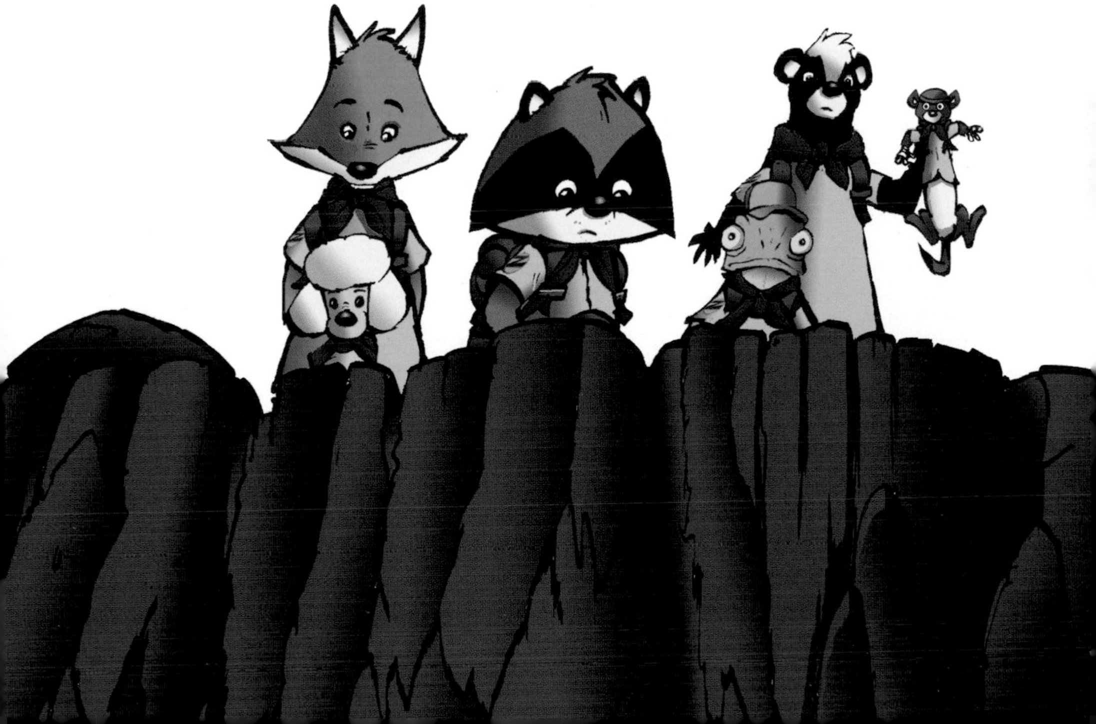

Tongue Twisters

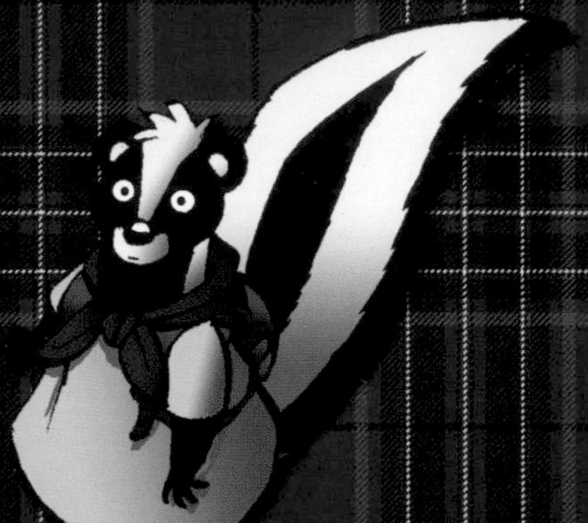

Musky must musk—to say,
"Nay!" is just mush.
One must not fuss or she
will blush and say,
"I must musk!"

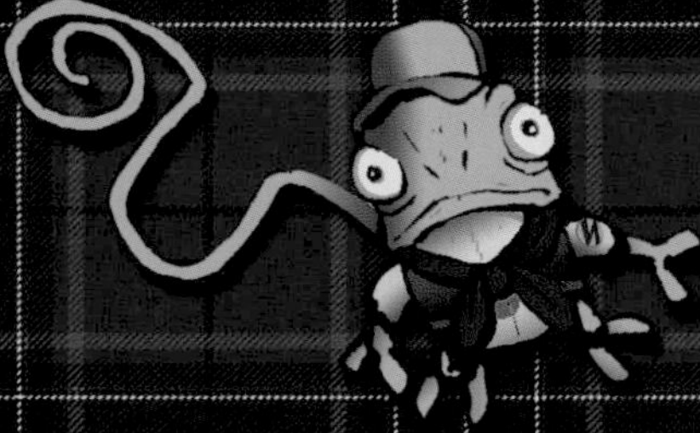

Shifty, all in green and
unseen, finds some pines,
sifts for nutty finds, pines
for fine food but instead,
unfed, shifts colors to red.

Billy Stuart visits Madame Crab's Chocolate Store
Can I have a chockfull chuck wagon of chocolate
crawfish for six hundred cents?
Six hundred cents? Six hundred cents? That makes
no sense! But for six hundred and six cents, you'll
be sent home with a shockingly chockfull chuck
wagon of chocolate chews instead!

Chapter 14

Daemon-Bat!

"What should we do now, Billy Stuart?" asks Shifty.

"Um..."

My *intuition* had almost caused all of us Zintrepids to plunge into a void! The crevasse looks like a gaping jaw ready to devour us. A jaw as big and **wide** as a highway. Impossible to jump across. Maybe we could order FrouFrou to try to jump over the abyss, so we can evaluate the distance we need to cross? I push the idea aside—I don't want to upset Foxy.

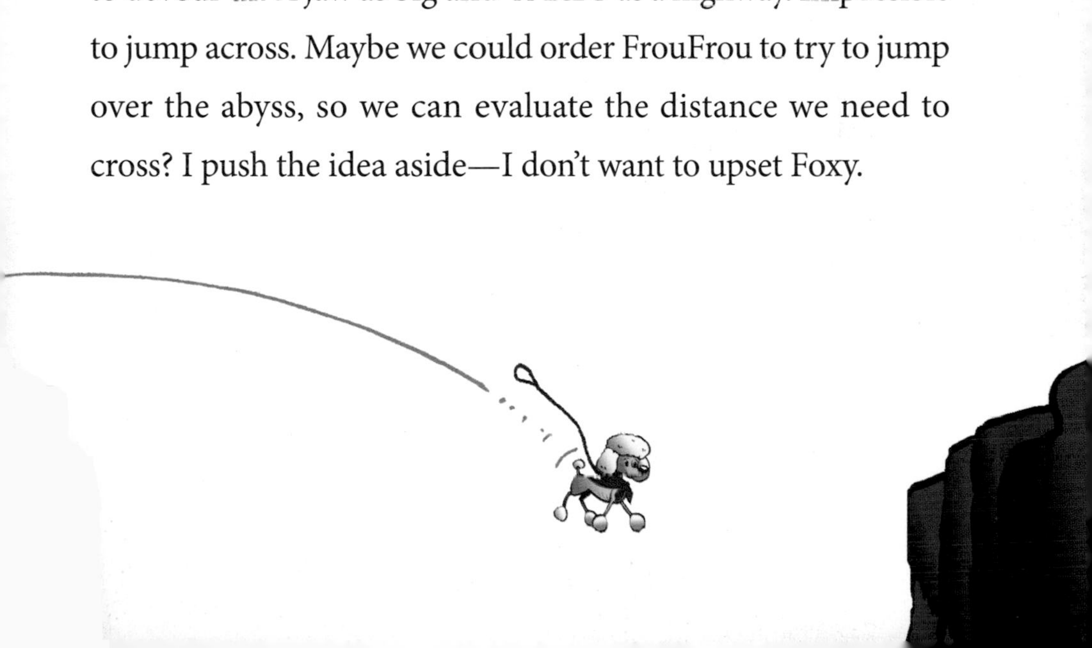

Shifty leans out over the void. You can't see the bottom. Musky shines her flashlight down, but the beam doesn't even penetrate the darkness. Yeti drops a stone and **waits. . . waits. . . and waits**.

"No sound," says the weasel.

"No bottom," adds the chameleon.

"That must go all the way to the center of the Earth," notes the fox.

"Troop! This way!" I say, pointing to a little path a hundred meters to our left.

SCRiiiiiii!!!

We had almost forgotten about that! As we approach a narrow stone bridge suspended over the chasm, we see something.

"There it is!" Foxy points.

The **strange creature** is holding itself ten meters above the ground.

"It's not Batman," says Shifty sadly.

"It's not a *bat*," says Musky, who is terrified of whatever it is.

The creature seems much more *daemon* than *bat*. It is the size of an adult human. Its **ARMS** and **LEGS** are separate from its **WINGS**. Its **HANDS** and **FEET** have claws. It has a bald **HEAD**, huge **EARS** and fiery **EYES**.

What is this? It's not exactly a bat, it's not exactly a human—it might be a vampire bat! Or maybe a daemon-bat!

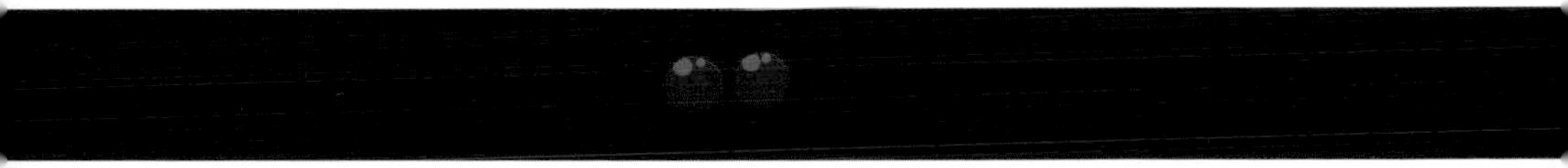

The daemon-bat bares **FORMIDABLE TEETH** that could cut us into pieces. Then suddenly it zooms upward and lets loose a bunch of guano, as if to make itself lighter. The substance lands in Musky's face, who is disgusted and bellows:

"Arghhhhh!"

Foxy hands the skunk a tissue to clean the goop off. It isn't big enough. The fox looks at me.

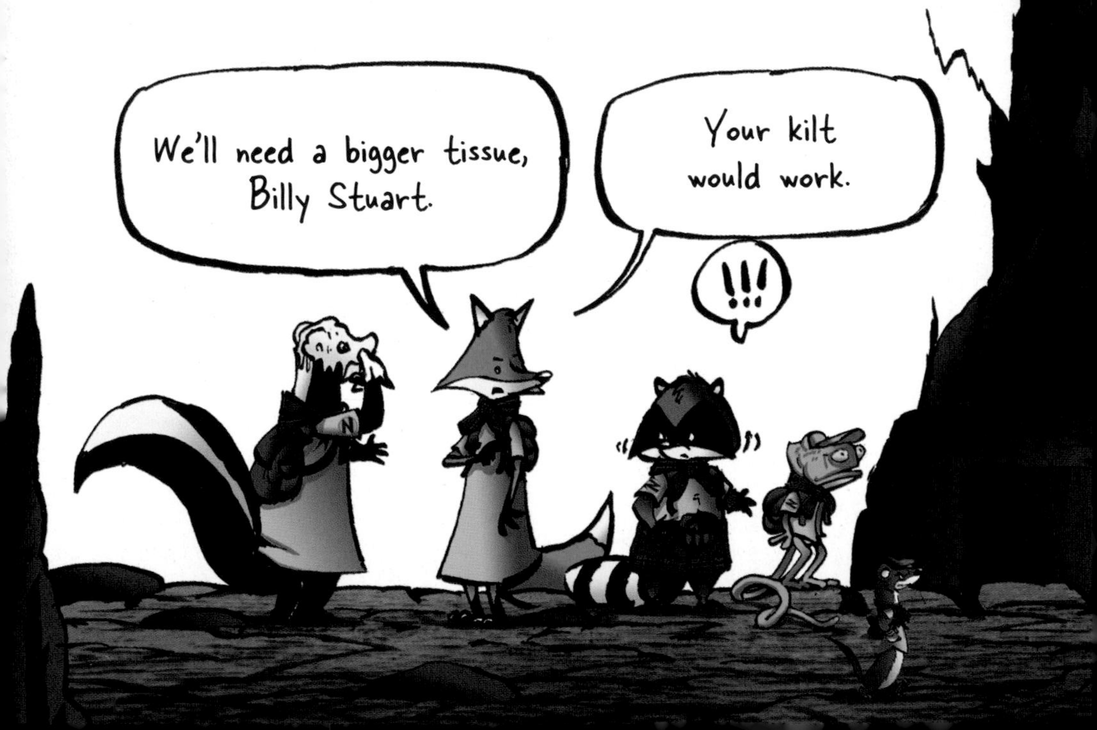
We'll need a bigger tissue, Billy Stuart.
Your kilt would work.
!!!

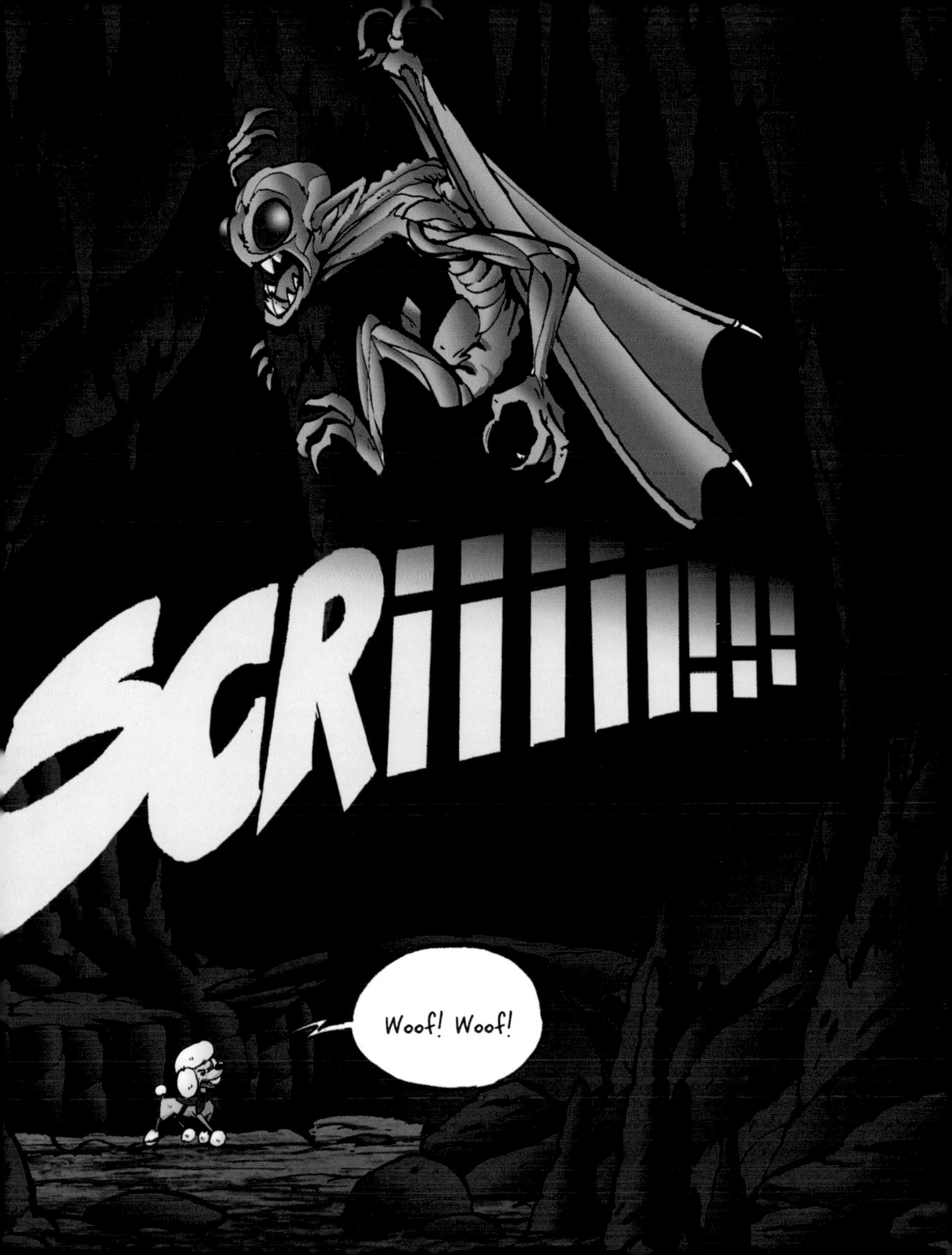
SCRiiiii!!!
Woof! Woof!

"OUT OF THE QUESTION! I am never without my kilt. And the guano would stain it."

"Selfish," mutters Musky.

"We won't look, Billy Stuart—we promise," says Shifty, chuckling.

"I know you too well," I say, offended.

SCRiiiiii!!!

We are wasting precious seconds arguing over this.

TROOP! ONWARD! "To the stone bridge!"

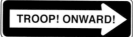

A Bridge-Quake

If the crevasse we are facing is the width of a highway, the **STONE BRIDGE** that crosses it is just a teeny tiny sidewalk. With the void on either side, I have the impression that the sidewalk at some point gets as narrow as a plank, or even a wire.

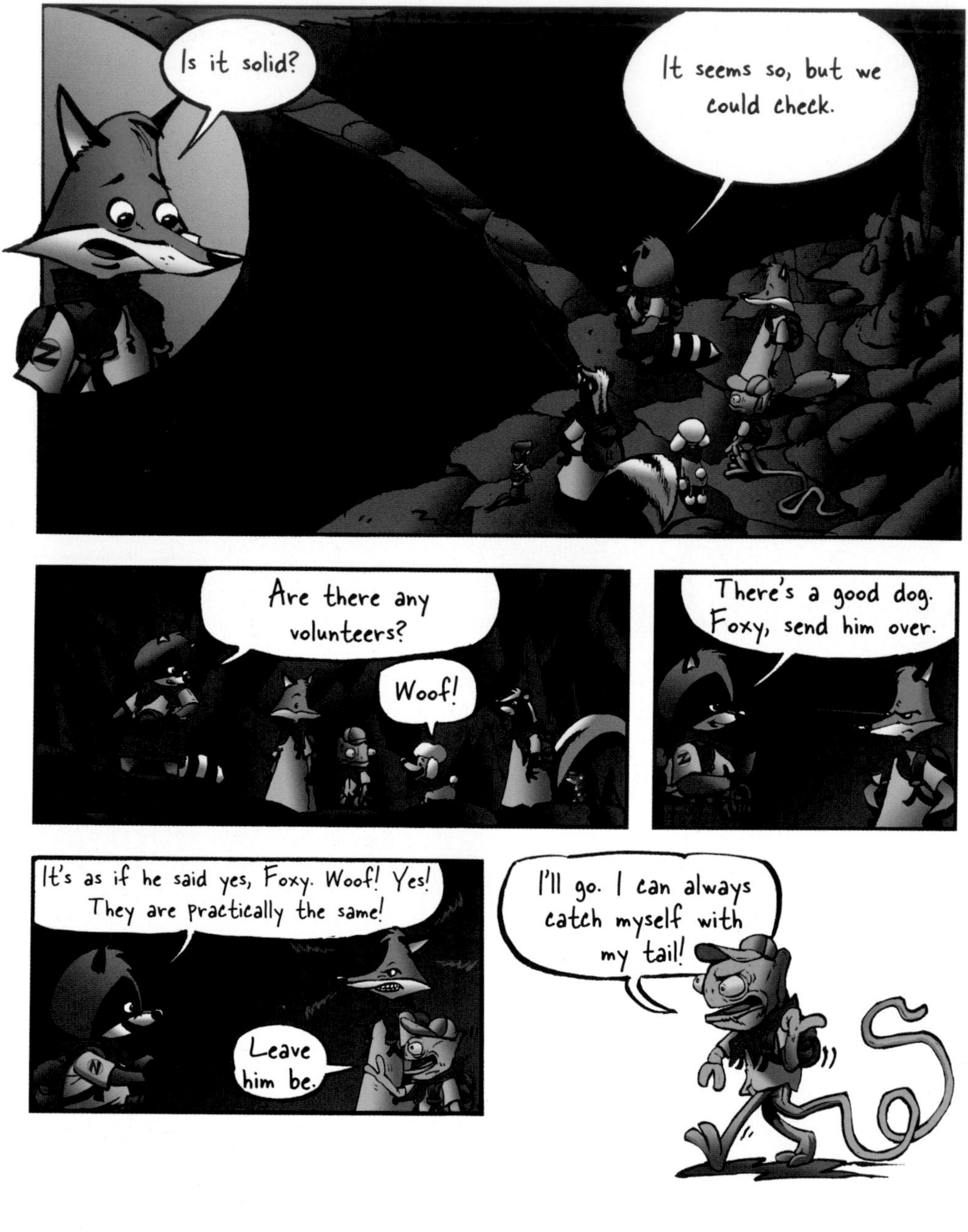
Is it solid?
It seems so, but we could check.
Are there any volunteers?
Woof!
There's a good dog. Foxy, send him over.
It's as if he said yes, Foxy. Woof! Yes! They are practically the same!
Leave him be.
I'll go. I can always catch myself with my tail!

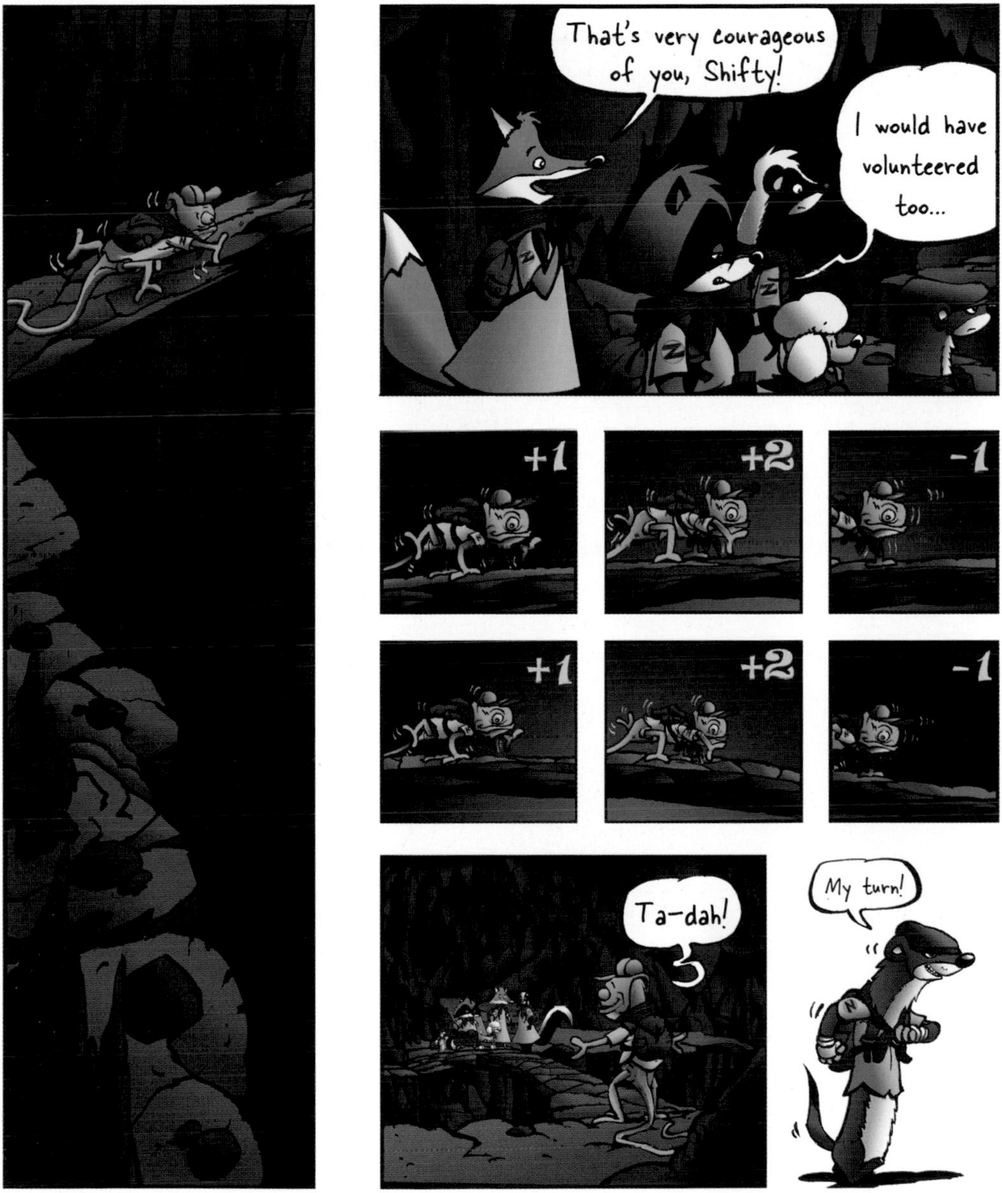
That's very courageous of you, Shifty!
I would have volunteered too...
+1
+2
-1
+1
+2
-1
Ta-dah!
My turn!

The weasel copies Shifty's position, getting on all fours, and does an odd dance across the spindly bridge. He joins the chameleon on the other side, safe and sound.

The poodle **barks** and tries to launch himself, ready for his turn. So impatient!

"You could let him go all by himself, Foxy."

She gives me a stern look.

"I prefer to go with him, Billy Stuart," she says curtly.

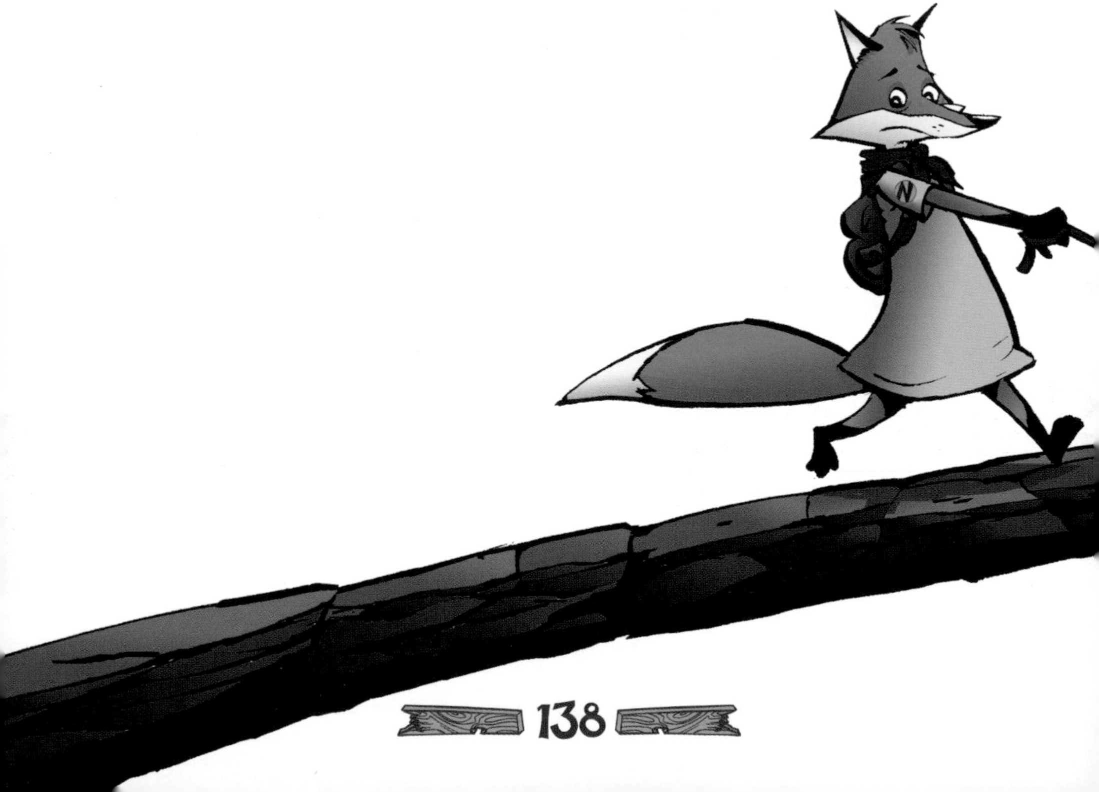

The leash is s̲t̲r̲e̲t̲c̲h̲e̲d̲ to the point of breaking.
FrouFrou leaps forward, oblivious to the danger beneath him.
One sudden movement or misstep and he would plunge into
the void, dragging Foxy with him.

I scream:

"Stupid pooch!"

And the echo responds:

...ooch...ooch...ooch...

SCRIiiiiij!!!

"BE CAREFUL, FOXY!"

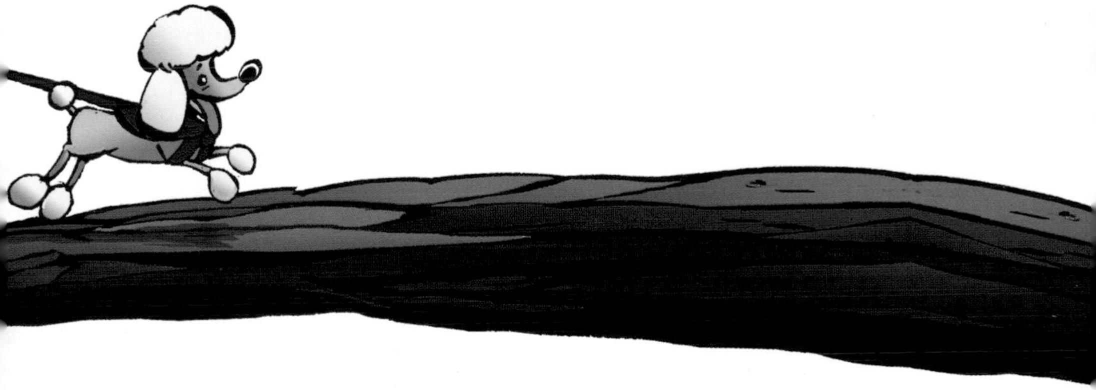

My warning sounds like an explosion. The daemon-bat surges in from nowhere and flies **THREATENINGLY** over the fox, who dodges it by flattening herself against the bridge. But the creature seizes FrouFrou in flight. There is a violent tug-of-war between Foxy and the winged beast. How long before the leash snaps?

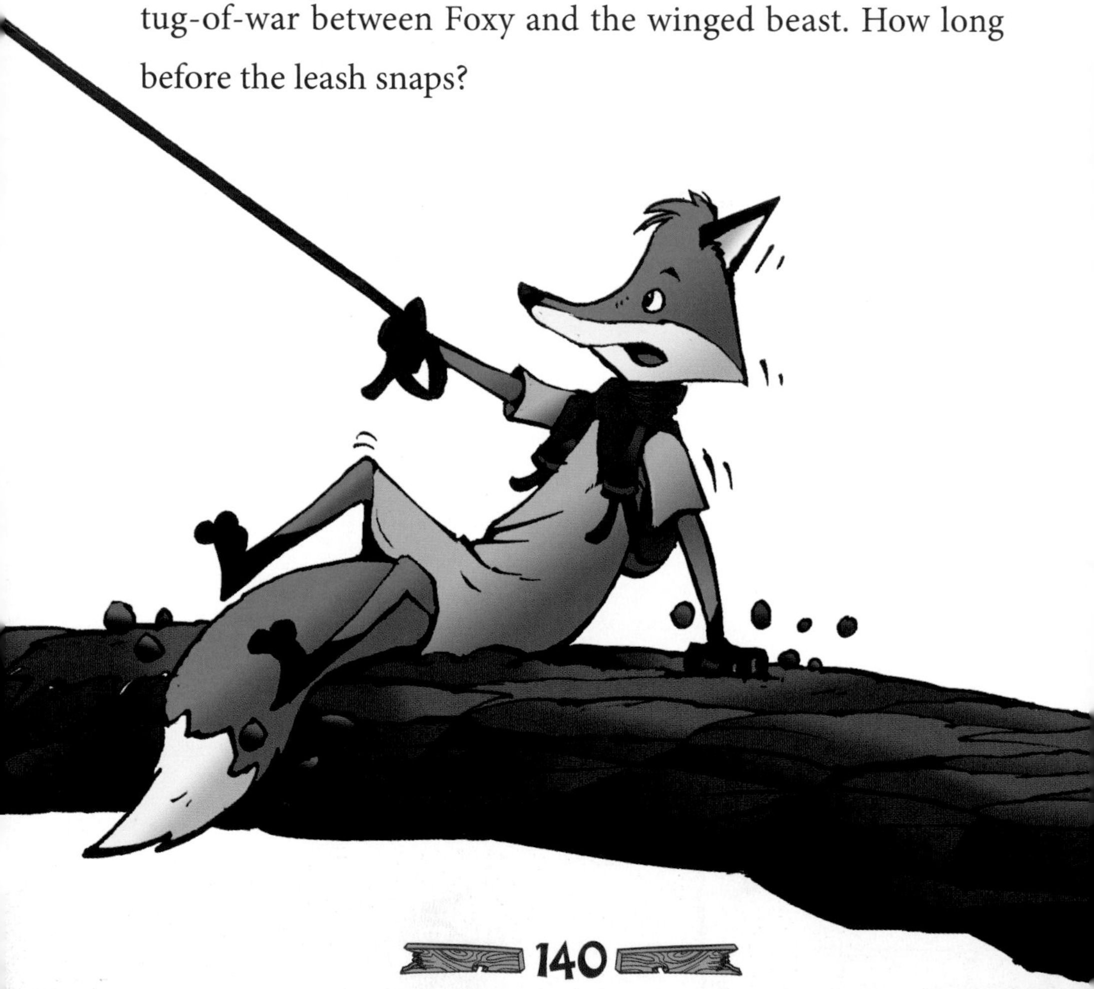

The daemon-bat is vigorously beating its wings, dragging the fox to the edge of the **BRIDGE**. Soon Foxy won't have a choice. She'll have to let go of the poodle to save her own skin.

"Let him go, Foxy!" I say, immediately regretting my words.

The dog trembles in the claws of the monster. Shifty risks the collapse of the bridge and a fall into the abyss himself and runs to help Foxy. It's useless—the daemon-bat is **TOO STRONG** for them.

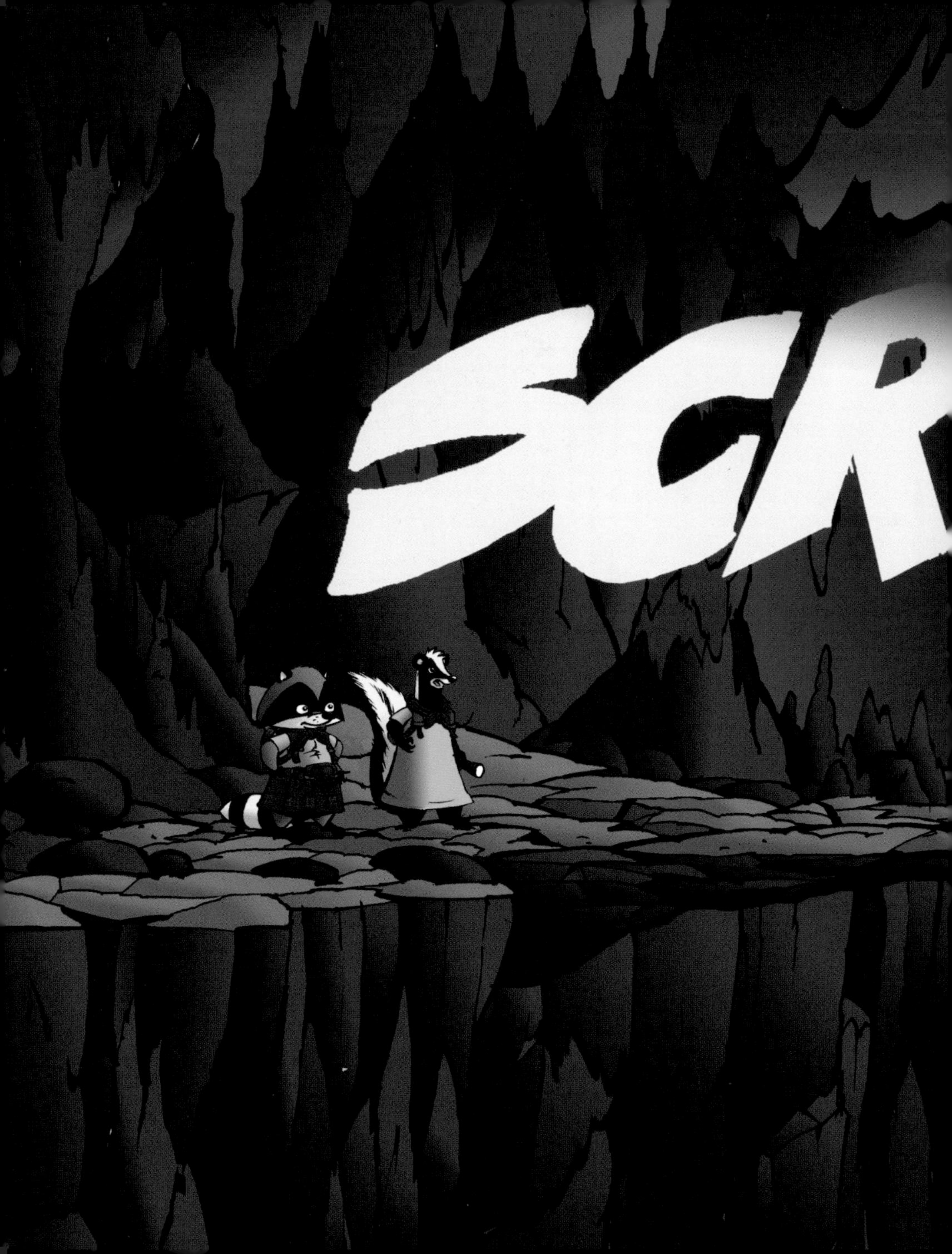
SCR

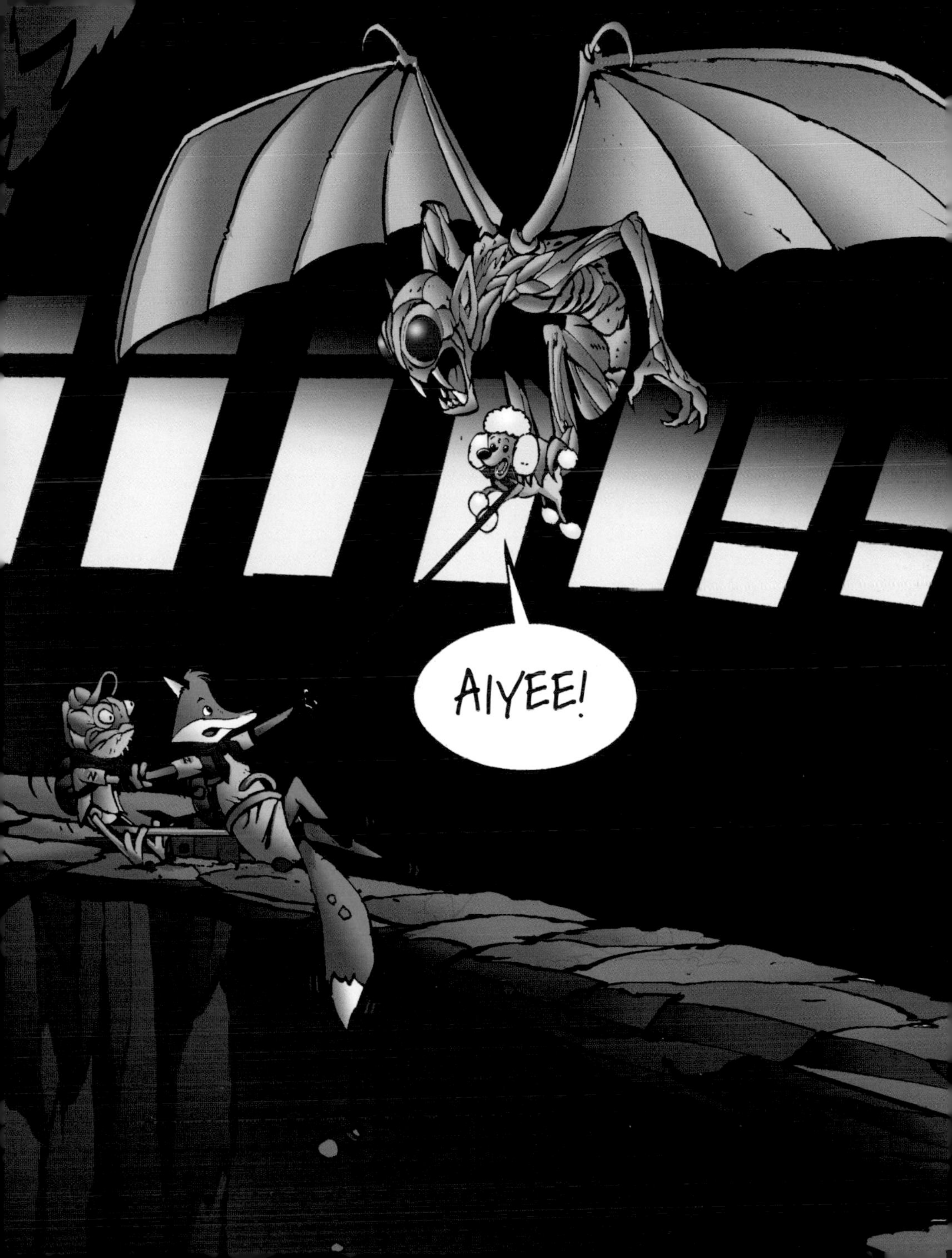
AIYEE!

"Let go of him, you dirty guano factory!" shouts Musky.

My brain speeds up: cave…bat…darkness…light—yes! Light!

I get Musky's flashlight and shine it in the daemon-bat's face.

Blinded, the creature tries to protect its eyes. It can't help but let go of the poodle. Then it flies off toward the cavern's vaulted ceiling.

The unexpected release of tension on the leash throws Foxy and Shifty off balance on the bridge. The shock of it almost sends them over the edge. The leash slips out of Foxy's hands.

FrouFrou starts to falllll, letting out a long howl.

Instantly Shifty reacts. He hooks his tail over the bridge, plunges into the abyss and sticks out his tongue, grabbing the dog in the nick of time.

“I…ve…im!”

“He has him! He has him!” Foxy translates.

Coming back up is a strange balancing act for the chameleon and FrouFrou, as they swing back and forth like a pendulum, cheered on by Foxy’s cries of joy.

“Bravo, Shifty! Now we rewind…”

Like a fish at the end of a line, the dog is brought safely back up to the stone bridge.

Musky and I join them. FrouFrou, like nothing has happened, dances on his hind legs, so happy to see us.

What about me? Is no one going to congratulate me on my genius idea?
Yes. Bravo!

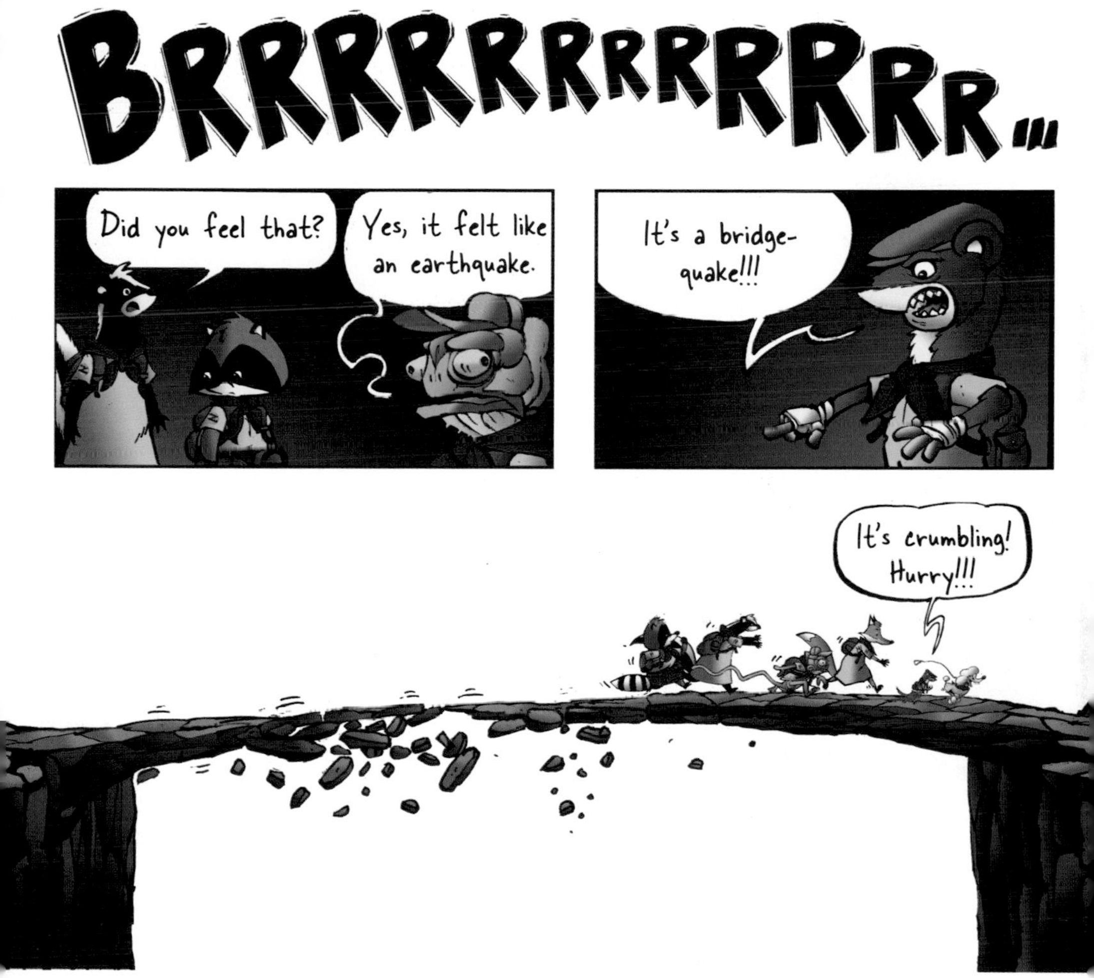
BRRRRRRRRRRRRR...
Did you feel that?
Yes, it felt like an earthquake.
It's a bridge-quake!!!
It's crumbling! Hurry!!!

We rush, single file, toward the side of the bridge that is still intact. I am the last in the line, and the bridge is crumbling behind me.

"**HURRY UP!!!!!**"

Am I going to fall backward into the void before reaching the edge?

The other Zintrepids reach the other side. I am the only one left, just a few meters from safety.

TOO LATE! The bridge crumbles beneath my feet. I stretch out my arms and, in a last-ditch effort, hurl myself forward. My fingers grip the cliff. Though my fingers are agile, they are not very strong. I feel myself sliding. I can't hold on. This is it! I fall toward $\mathbf{infiniiiiityyyyyyyyy}$...

Two **hands**, Foxy's and Musky's, grab mine. Abruptly my fall stops. Using my **toes**, I press myself against the wall to climb back up.

Out of breath and tired, I sit on the ground and gush, "Thank you, thank you, thank you."

Another **SCRIIIII** echoes through the cavern. We jump up and start moving immediately.

"So long, daemon-bat!" yells Shifty.

A PUZZLE

On a nice summer day, the Zintrepids walked in single file. To protect themselves from the sun's rays, each carried a small sun visor. They all drank a beverage, ate a snack and walked beside an animal. Yes, even Billy Stuart!

To solve this puzzle, you will have to determine for each of the friends:

COLOR OF SUN VISOR (red, blue, white, green or yellow)	ACCOMPANYING ANIMAL (grasshopper, rabbit, poodle, fish, cat)	THE BEVERAGE (water, lemonade, milk, juice, tea)	THE SNACK (licorice, ice cream, crawfish, popcorn, candy)	ORDER IN WHICH THEY WALKED (1st, 2nd, 3rd, 4th, 5th)
	 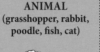			

Here are your clues:

1. Billy Stuart is at the center of the group. He's wearing a red sun visor.

2. Foxy is walking the cat and is at the end of the line.

3. Musky is drinking a lemonade under his blue sun visor.

4. The green sun visor is before the white sun visor in line.

5. The one with the green sun visor is drinking juice and is behind the red sun visor in line.

6. The one who is walking the poodle is eating a crawfish. Clue: He says all the time, "This is not my dog!"

7. The one who is wearing the yellow sun visor is eating licorice.

8. The one in the middle of the line is drinking milk.

9. Shifty is wearing a yellow sun visor. He is at the head of the line.

10. The one who is eating ice cream is behind the one who is walking the grasshopper.

11. The one who is walking the rabbit is behind the licorice eater.

12. The one who is eating candy is drinking tea.

13. Yeti is eating popcorn.

14. Shifty is in front of the one who is wearing the blue sun visor.

15. The one who is having ice cream is behind the one drinking water.

16. And, lastly, someone is carrying a fish!?!

Solution on page 159.

Chapter 16

Back in the Open Air

My intuition, despite the bridge episode, is right this time. The cave that I described as a **GIGANTIC** and **INTERMINABLE** gymnasium is not without end. As we continue on, the walls close in, almost like a funnel. And at the end of the funnel there is a light. A real one! The light of day. The light of the Sun.

We **cheer** as we exit into the open air.

"We win!" rejoices Foxy, cheered on by FrouFrou's barking.

But our **celebrations** are short-lived. We are not at the foot of the mountain, where we thought we would be, but on a plateau overlooking the valley below.

"This is not the valley of the Kanuks," observes Musky.

Should I tell my friends what I think has happened?

It's better that they learn the truth sooner rather than later. They already have so many questions.

I take my grandfather's notebook out of my purse.

The purse is a little leather sack that is attached to a strap or chain worn around the hips. When we met, Billy Stuart used the word sporran, the traditional name for a kilt bag.

"Troop, when you have a Band-Aid on, do you prefer it to be ripped off quickly? Or **very slowlllllllly**?"

"With my lizard skin, it doesn't really bother me either way," says Shifty.

"Quickly!" agree Musky, Foxy and Yeti.

"That's what I was thinking. So get ready—I am about to rip it off. I think we have just **traveled through time**. My grandfather found a passageway in the cavern that allowed him to change eras—and places, as you can see. This is no longer **Kanuks Forest**."

There is a **loud** silence. Should I have told them **slowlllllllly**?

My friends look at each other in disbelief. My fingers rub the leather notebook, lingering on the Y engraved in the upper right corner, the signature of the object's owner.

I look out at the horizon.

"Troop, we are…elsewhere. Where and when? I don't know. But under our feet, there is a whole **NEW WORLD** to discover."

SEARCH AND FIND

Can you spot these items in the book?

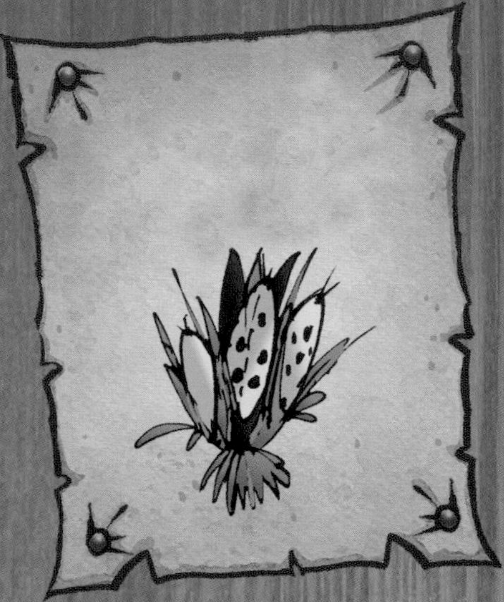

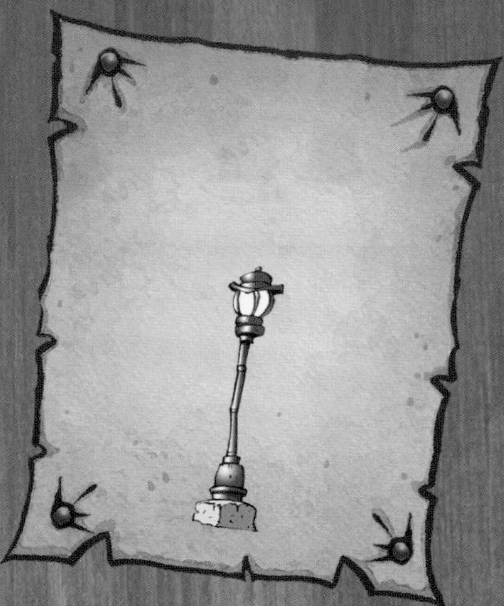

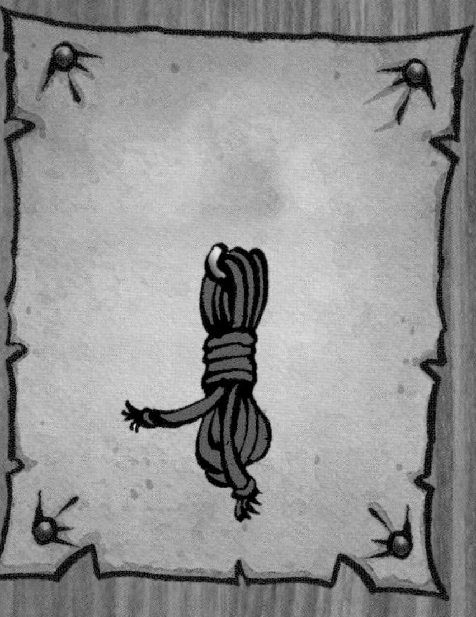

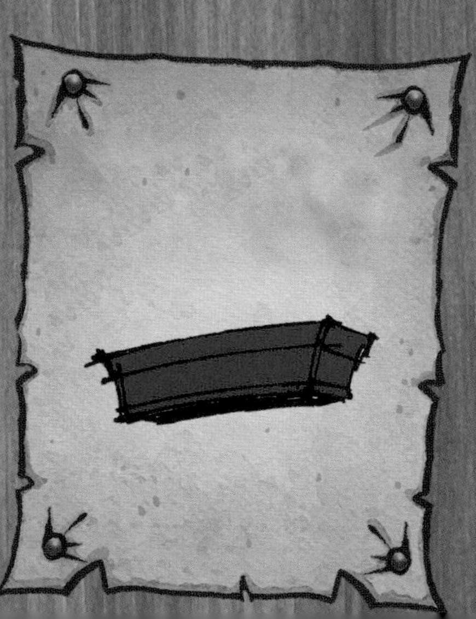

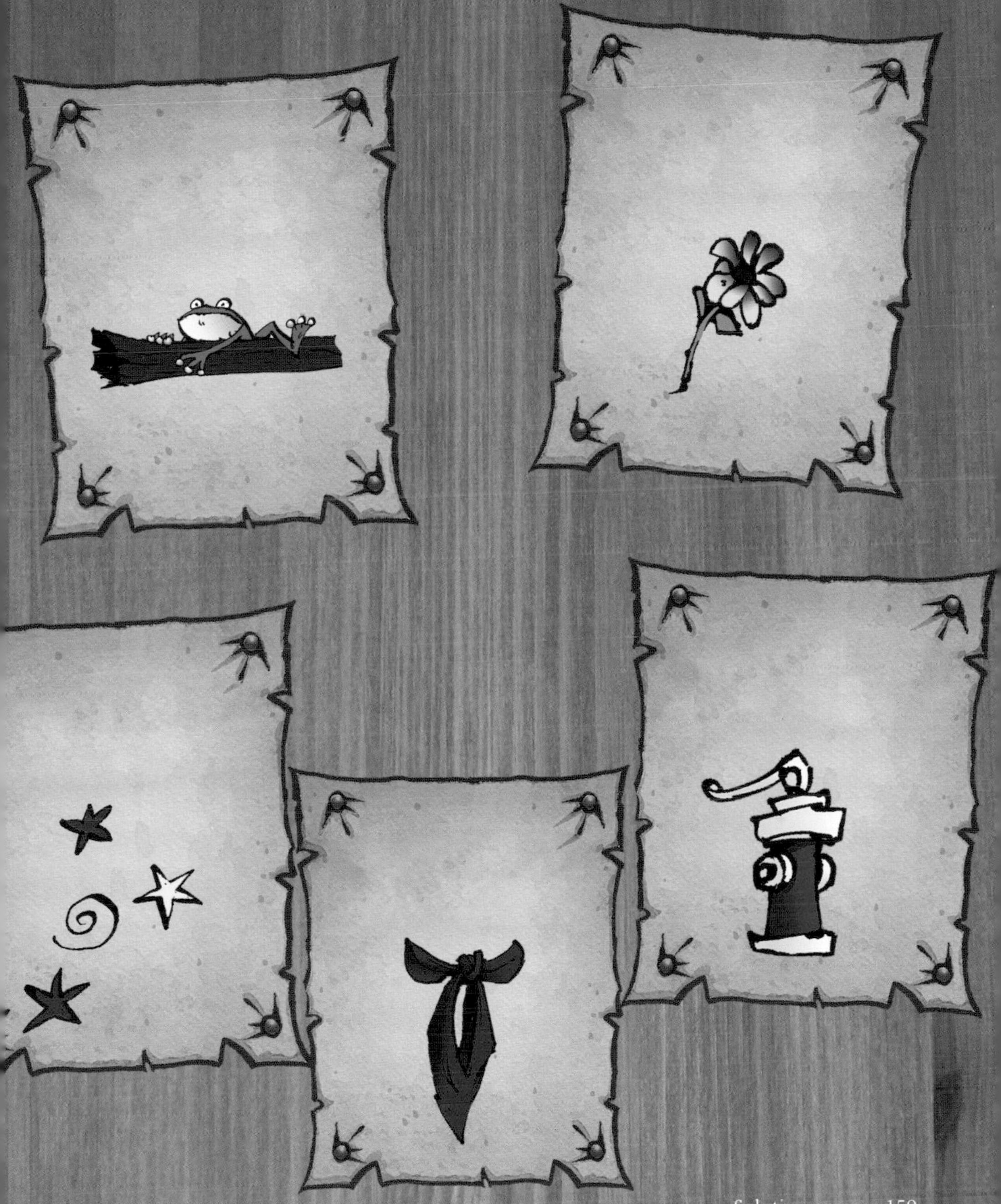

Solution on page 159.

SOLUTIONS

TOPSY-TURVY (PAGE 74)
THIS GAME HAS MANY SOLUTIONS.
HERE IS ONE:

BEAR-BEAD-BEND-BAND-HAND

WHO AM I? (PAGE 94)
1. ANSWER: PURSE (PURR-SSS!)
2. ANSWER: CHAMELEON (KAA-ME-LEE-ON)
3. ANSWER: ASTOUNDED (ASS-TOWN-DEAD)

PUZZLE TABLE (PAGE 150)

	1st	2nd	3rd	4th	5th
CHARACTER	SHIFTY	MUSKY	BILLY STUART	YETI	FOXY
COLOR OF SUN VISOR	YELLOW	BLUE	RED	GREEN	WHITE
ANIMAL	GRASS-HOPPER	RABBIT	POODLE	FISH	CAT
BEVERAGE	WATER	LEMONADE	MILK	JUICE	TEA
SNACK	LICORICE	ICE CREAM	CRAWFISH	POPCORN	CANDY

SEARCH AND FIND (PAGES 156-157)

CORN COBS: PAGE 36

LAMPPOST: PAGE 15

FROG: PAGE 84

FLOWER: PAGE 36

ROPE: PAGE 42

FLOWER BOX: PAGE 26

STARS: PAGE 115

BILLY'S SCARF: PAGE 42

FIRE HYDRANT: PAGE 8

A prolific author, Alain M. Bergeron has written over 250 children's books. He devotes himself exclusively to writing and leading school workshops. His inexhaustible imagination has made him a fixture in children's literature, and he has received many awards and accolades. Alain lives in Victoriaville, Quebec.

Multitalented, self-taught illustrator and cartoonist Samuel Parent, better known by the pen name Sampar, possesses a lively imagination that draws viewers into worlds that are moving, wacky and sometimes even mythical. He lives in Victoriaville, Quebec.

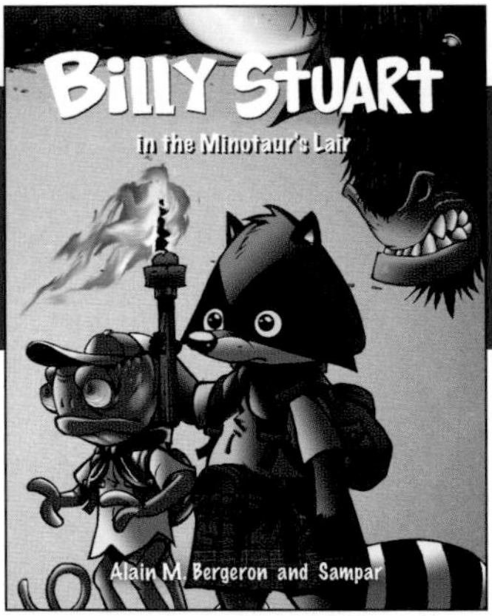

BILLY STUART
in the Minotaur's Lair
Alain M. Bergeron and Sampar

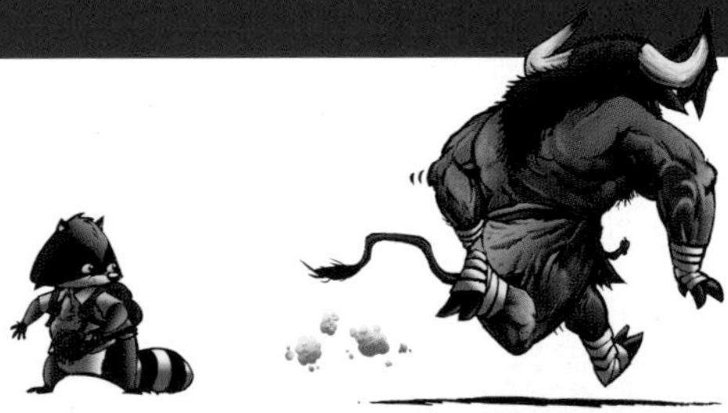